The Org

K.J. HENNESSY

First published in 2023
by K.J. Hennessy, NSW Australia
'Kamili Club Publishing'
ABN 97 735 188 763

Typeset & Cover Design: Nada Backovic
Editor: Katie Kearns
Original Cover Art 'While the city sleeps' by © Scott Marsh, 2019

A catalogue record for this book is available from the National Library of Australia.

ISBN 978 0 6457688 0 0 (paperback)
ISBN 978 0 6457688 1 7 (ebook)

Dedicated to 5-year-old me.

You did it.

This book was written on Worimi, Gadigal and Awabakal lands.
The author and publisher acknowledge the Traditional Owners and
recognise their continuing connection to land, waters and culture.

We pay respects to their Elders past, present and emerging, and hope
to share connection to land, waters and culture for a meaningful and
sustainable future.

We acknowledge the split in our identity, and wish to heal it.

Sovereignty was never ceded.

Notes On Styling & Slang

Certain words in this book may come across as unfamiliar. They're likely slang.

Abbreviations may include losing the 'g' in -ing suffixes (e.g. stingin = stinging) and combining words (e.g. gonna = going to / kinda = kind of).

Bacch uses '&' instead of 'and', unless it's at the beginning of a sentence, or if it follows a comma.

Cristina doesn't use ampersands.

Now the serpent was more crafty than any beast of the field which the LORD God had made. And he said to the woman, "Indeed, has God said, 'You shall not eat from any tree of the garden'?"

Genesis 3:1

Bacch

I first met Cristina when she came for a rental inspection. I'd forgotten about the rental inspection.

I awoke on the couch, sweating, to her knock at the door. I'd been dreaming that Protectors were hunting me across a deep, ancient desert. Wild & vivid. It was the third year of summer.

Looking around, there were pretzels & icing splotches & finger bun crumbs everywhere. *Ah.* Bianca the Baker had been over last night. She always came over after work with the day's leftovers. Always too much sugar. There is a finite number of donuts & finger buns a human being can eat, and I'm merely human. Bianca was not merely human. She was a 6-foot-tall goddess of water-polo-playing proportions. She moved her body with smouldering precision. Ex-dancer. The cutest lil nose. Steely eyes.

Sydney was overrun by people clambering to live in boxes with views of other people's boxes. Prices had never been higher. I'd considered living in a van before finding this old place in Surry Hills, countless jumbled storeys of stained brick; beat up, haphazard living. Tiny green leaves peeked out from cracks in the walls. I had some plants that I watered. It was home.

The other bedroom had been empty for a week. To cover rent, I'd tried trading in cryptocurrencies, but still didn't really know what they were. I was also tutoring kids, and selling Bianca's second-hand goods to other residents in the building. Cheers, Bianca.

Whoever Cristina was, she would not appreciate all this sweet debris. But what choice do you have when she's knocking at your door?

I checked my phone for the time. Notifications claimed The Org had reinstated the death penalty in Australia, even wheeled out the King to announce it. Too early in the arvo for that shit. Perhaps these were just more false reports from real news anchors, fake news about real events that never happened.

I wiped my eyes, put some pants on, and opened the door.

I'm in trouble.

Our soldiers blow each other into bloody oblivion across ravaged foreign landscapes while I greet this fair lady at my door. The world has never been fair. She tucked her long, light-brown hair behind an ear. A white summer dress hung off her shoulders. Her smile was soft but her eyes were cautious.

"Sorry," I said. "There's been a food fight."

She frowned a bit. "Are you ... *Bacch*? Am I saying that right?"

"Yeah. Cristina?"

"Yep. Can I still see the apartment?"

"There's cake & shit everywhere."

"And ... and *what*?"

"Oh, no, not actual ... just cake."

"Look, Bacch, I'm here to see the place. Please?"

I stepped aside for her.

"You weren't lying about the mess," she said.

"Great apartment otherwise."

It really was, but it was scheduled for demolition – though no date had been given. Developers owned it, so I advertised through flatmate websites & not an agent. Real estate agents just want to fuck you over. Why does everyone just want to fuck you over?

The kitchen was actually quite clean. Cristina remarked upon it. Maybe it would be the saving grace. It looked out onto Central Station, a few IV trees, lots of humans. The skyscrapers were melting like sticks of steel butter.

San Pedro cacti grew in pots in the far corner of the living room. Some of the stems had grown so much they climbed out the window, stretching up to the sky. There was a beat three-seater couch, a coffee table with an incense holder smothered in soft ash, a decent stereo system, fluffy carpet that massaged between your toes, and bizarre art splattered across the walls, painted by old friends or artists needing quick cash. A few years ago, a friend gifted me this central piece here, after some brief intimacies. Since then, he's been an Archibald Prize finalist for his surreal portraits of Org Civil Servants with split tongues, bifurcated like a snake's – though I heard he stopped painting since the Protectors visited his home. I could get a good price on the gift, but I'd rather keep it: a fat, sleepy koala nestled against a gumtree shaped like a crucifix, with a bushfire raging below. Thick chunky strokes & slabs of bright paint. Beautiful.

Cristina looked at it with strange, thoughtful eyes, touching the cross around her neck. Beautiful.

But I ushered her along into the spare room. A bedframe was still there, plus some drawers.

"What happened to the previous tenant?" Cristina asked.

"She got deported. The new immigration laws."

"She was a terrorist?"

"No. She was a student."

I was hungover & it was getting worse.

God, I need a job.

Cristina looked out the bedroom window, then back to me. "Why are you called 'Bacch', Bacch?"

"Ah ... Mum & Dad thought they were naming me after the genius composer. High expectations. But they spelt it wrong, with two Cs. Like Bacchus."

"Who?"

"A Roman god. Also kinda high expectations."

She tilted her head. "A dead god?"

3

"Yes, well ... at least we know that gods can die."

"Hmm ..." She peered out the bedroom window, across the city. "So, what was this dead god all about?"

My headache thumped. I was too thirsty for this. "Bacchus was ... um ... like the Greek Dionysus. God of wine & grape harvests, of fruit & fertility, festivals & theatre, nature, cultivation, ritual madness, religious ecstasy, insanity ... all the same thing."

Cristina said nothing, just touched her necklace, the cross. We shuffled along. She checked out the bathroom, moving stiffly, like she wasn't in touch with herself.

"Did you write this?" she asked, pointing at the mirror. I approached to see *fuck you* scrawled in whipped cream & sticky jam on the glass. Perfect for an inspection. Cheers, Bianca.

"Nah, that was ... a friend. Otherwise, what do you think of the place?"

"You need to clean up." She rubbed her hand through the *fuck*, smeared & scrambled it.

We said our goodbyes, that we'd contact each other in the next day or two. She walked away from me, down those creaky stairs. I never expected to see her again.

My bladder bulged. I ran to the bathroom, past the defaced *fuck you* mirror. My piss was pink. All those donuts, cheers, Bianca. Cheers to you.

Cristina

The trees are strange here, not like in the country.

Walking into my first induction day at The Org, I noticed these huge pulsing veins of sap running all over the trunks, between and beneath the bark. The trees lined the pathway into the massive entrance of the building, in the Barangaroo precinct. Tiny IV lines fed the roots from a small, locked metal box next to each one. I'd never seen anything quite like it.

I was still staying in a hostel in Potts Point (I think it used to be called Kings Cross, before the curfews began). After work, I visited another real estate agent, a little bald madman. Each time I asked the rental costs for a property he screamed, "One ... million ... dollars!!"

"Oh ... per week?"

"Oh yes."

"Ok ... and how about this property in Ultimo?"

"One ... *million* ... dollars!!"

"Ok ... and this one here in Redfern?"

"*One ... million ... DOLLARS!!*"

"Are they all a million?"

"No. This one, the bedroom used to be a hallway. Good girth. For a hallway. $550 per week plus utilities. Lots of competition for this one, so get in quick."

His laughter chased me out of the office and down the street.

I made my way to the train station afterwards, considering my options, fiddling with the tiny cross around my neck, between my collarbones. The Surry Hills apartment was by far the cheapest I'd found.

Close enough to The Org. It was … messy. The tenant seemed a tad eccentric. Handsome, in an afflicted way. Odd name. The kitchen was clean, at least. The previous occupant got deported.

I wonder what happened to her?

I tapped my Org ID card at the turnstile and descended the grimy escalator, down into the depths of the city. My breathing was shallow – I could taste the hot, trapped air of the tunnels.

Mum and Dad wouldn't want me living with a boy. They thought I was at The Org dorms. Nope. It felt like the right thing for me, to live independently, at least a little. But I was lying to my parents. *How can something be wrong, yet feel right? Or be right, yet feel wrong?* The Youth Program inductions were already intense enough, and it was only the first day. They made us repeat phrases about The Org and our country, to help us through such contradictions. One in particular came to mind as the dilapidated train screeched to a halt at the platform.

The honour of the Civil Servant is vested in his ability to execute conscientiously the order of superior authorities.

So, as long as I behaved 'conscientiously' at The Org, the superior authority, could I make my own choices about where I live?

Is a parent a superior authority? Or are we one and the same, like Jesus and the Holy Father?

Living out of home, everything seemed open to interpretation.

There were recruitment ads for the Program everywhere, even on the underground train, staring at me from every wall. I looked forward to finally becoming part of something, experiencing something.

The youth are the future. We are the future.

The honour of the Civil Servant. The order of superior authorities.

Two Org Scouts sat nearby, whispering to each other. Young girls, dark blue plaid skirts, white collared shirts, black polished shoes, red lipstick. Their eyes darted across passengers, inspecting them, as they whispered. The Org crest was emblazoned on their shirts, the kangaroo and emu. They each held a large, white Bible. Their eyes caught mine.

6

The youth are the future.

I looked away. Across from me, a man began to scream, his eyes and fists clenched. No one would help him. I approached while everyone else looked at their screens, earphones in. I even heard a snigger. The Scouts stood and moved to a different carriage.

"Sir? Are you ok?" I said this at a slight distance.

He stopped screaming and looked at me. The skin around his eyes was cracked.

"Are you ok?" I asked again.

He shook his head. The train slowed. It was my stop.

"Everything will be ok," I said.

And I walked off the train.

Making my way through the station, up to Victoria Street, it all replayed in my mind. If we cared more about the misfortunes of others and laughed at our own, instead of the other way around, the world would be a heaps happier place. But I couldn't really do anything.

Is the human psyche collectively damaged?

Praise The Org.

During our induction tour earlier, they showed us what was below the ground floor of The Org – a grandiose chamber.

"This is New Parliament House," said our guide, dressed in red, white and blue, like the Scouts, like our flag. "It includes the Senate, and the House of Servants. They rebuilt it here as a foundation for the building, because our laws are the foundation for a proper society. It is also reinforced to double as a bunker, stocked with years of non-perishables and wifi, in case nuclear war finally occurs."

"Sir?" I asked.

"Yes?"

"What's below this level?"

The guide hesitated, eyeing me. Then he grinned.

"Why, that's where The Org keeps the troublemakers."

Some inductees whispered to each other behind me.

"I'm joking, of course!" The guide clapped his hands together. "Now, upstairs to the skybridge!"

Everything will be ok.

Bacch

I was not ready to hear romance songs on the crackling café radio, or the loud laughter of strangers in love, or sales pitches for nine-day gym membership trials – but I hadn't eaten in a long time & this place was cheap & badly lit. In the window reflection, I saw I still had eyeliner on. Faces passed outside as if in a dream, each of wondrous potential & emotional faculty, yet gone in a glimpse. A city of strangers, all experiencing the same place, brushing each other in morning rush hour yet so far apart.

Oxford Street used to have rainbow flags all up & down it. Not anymore.

I didn't own a car but I'd borrowed my friend Hari's because he was in a K-hole most of the night, unable to interact. Ketamine isn't my kinda thing, but he enjoys it. We were all at Hari's friend's house party in Darlinghurst. Protectors came through briefly due to a noise complaint but it was too early for them to really do anything. DJs played in the living room. I was chatting to a guy, Alexis, long dark hair, good figure. Hari sank into a couch upstairs. It was a sesh. Later on, Alexis and I began to kiss, gently, when *bang* – Protectors kicked the front door off the hinges and burst through the house, knocking a girl's tooth out with a riot shield along the way. They raided the place, took every bit of stereo equipment in the house, even if it wasn't plugged in. They broke the beds, and someone's ribs. They used pepper spray to herd us out, coughing & crying, though Alexis & I avoided any direct hits. Hari never left the couch.

We walked back to Alexis's place nearby, a tiny terrace rental in Paddington. I slowed down. My heartbeat sped up. The lamp lights glowed from among the leaves of brush box trees along his street. He reached the door.

"I haven't been … with a guy, one on one, for a long while," I said.

"One on one?" he repeated with a smile, letting me walk through, locking the door behind us.

"My ex and I sometimes shared ourselves, together …"

"A girl?"

"Bianca. We started taking PrEP last year, all good there, but I don't really … douche."

"You're not a bottom?"

"On special occasions …"

"Isn't every occasion special?"

We laughed as he led me upstairs. It helped ease my nerves. At the door to his room, he turned and touched my forearms, slowly stepping close.

"I have a spare kit here. We can do everything, if you want. Do you want?"

I wasn't sure. I kissed him, delaying my response. Freshly shaven, with a solid jawline. Maybe *everything* wouldn't be so bad. I thought of Bianca. Our lips separated.

"Maybe we can just … I dunno," I said, looking away. My heartbeat was rising into my throat. I just wanted to walk out, leave, go home, like every other time, every other boy.

"Go snorkelling?" He said, still with his mischievous smile.

I laughed. "What even is that?"

So we stripped each other down & went snorkelling & made some noise & his housemates shouted to keep it down, which spoiled him just off the verge, so he stormed out, unclothed & sweaty, and the yelling between them got even louder. Later he slept & I couldn't. I got up to piss and found glitter on my cock. *Good morning, world.*

I roamed the unfamiliar house naked, found some delicious home-baked cookies someone had left out, probably not for me, but I'd missed dinner. Swallowed the last bit of fruit in the bowl & some wine from an abandoned glass on the bench, careful not to sip where the lipstick was. I left the terrace house in the rising sunlight, barefoot, shoes & socks in hand as I passed everyone setting up stalls for Paddington Markets. Humans starting their days while I was still trying to kill yesterday.

I made it back to the car just as a Parking Protector was about to issue a fine & official spanking. The Org owned everything, even the carparks. A whole section of footpath was crumbling as roots from a towering fig tree pushed up through the concrete. I tripped over one, walking around to the driver-side door. The car was covered in white & green bird shit, and sticky figs. Still, better than a parking fine. I stalled as I reversed – the back tyre was chocked against a giant root that had grown & burst through the tarmac.

The couple next to me at the café discussed the paperwork for their upcoming marriage. I closed my crumpled eyes, hiding them away.

Cupid is a cunt. I've never met a more sadistic baby.

I gotta get out of here.

Cristina

The hostel had hundreds of languages cross-firing at all times. It was music I understood nothing of, secret codes that delighted my ears. Except when slurred accents woke me in the shared bunkbed rooms, hours before I had to leave for The Org or another inspection.

Back home, when I couldn't sleep, I would walk around the backyard, naked but for my dressing robe, barefoot and bathed in moonlight. There were always snakes in the yard, but you couldn't often see them. I'd let the robe open, letting the breeze slip in, much of my young self exposed, feeling guilty yet enjoying the fear that someone might see me, that God could see me.

I had no words of beauty to describe my curves and dips and shapes. Only the knowledge that the flesh is sinful, that my exposed teenage body, at the beach or anywhere, would incite lust in others, would invite trouble. I would try to utter something poetic about my body, but all I had at my disposal was crudity, whatever I'd heard in schoolyard conversation. Anything else was denied to us. I would tighten the robe around me, tie my body back up, away from nature's touch, and return, restless, to bed.

Sleep was evasive at the hostel. One night I slipped out, barefoot, and wandered the streets, empty. All to myself. Relaxing in the silence of moonlight. But it wasn't silent and the moon was lost behind buildings and smog. Instead, the streetlights washed over the throbbing pavements and asphalt and parked cars and leaves of trees attached to IVs. There were always sirens, and this constant droning, machines ripping up roads and pipes.

They warn you against walking the streets alone at night. But I just want some air.

Everyone else seemed to need protection from the ground. I loved feeling it underfoot. Too hot for shoes anyway. Grass was scarce, just concrete and tar, kind of filthy actually, and the occasional bright crimson waratah flower bursting up from gaps and cracks, barely noticeable. I ran my hands across the bark of a few IV trees, ran my fingers through vines crawling up buildings, as if caressing someone's hair, touching to connect, leaves on fingertips, fingertips on lips –

Pain shot up my leg. Something cut me. Broken glass. I limped back to the hostel by myself, bare foot bleeding. A figure followed me a few blocks until I got inside and closed the door. No one else was around. I hopped through the building, leaving a trail of blood, until I reached the showers. I got naked in the fluorescent lights – curves and dips and shapes exposed – and sat under the running water, picking glass out of my skin, scrubbing the city from my toes, alone.

Bacch

I walked to the bakery on Crown Street where Bianca worked. I'd run out of bread, and wanted to see her. A group of eight Protectors with dogs stopped me along the way & searched me for twenty minutes. It took up the whole footpath, causing people to step around on to the road. The Protectors yelled at them to stay on the footpath, for their safety. I had nothing. They let me go with a warning.

Things could always be worse. Could be better, too.

The bakery had a line out the door. I walked past everyone to the front. Many wore face masks. Bianca didn't actually bake. She just made fruit juices & coffees & sold cocaine & pills to businesspeople & students. Particular customers would browse until Bianca was free, then chat with her, place an order for a cinnamon scroll or soy & linseed buns, pay, and leave. Customer satisfaction. Her sleight of hand was an art. The owners had no idea. She brought in more than anyone. They loved her. I loved her. But I love too easily.

Bianca came out back for a smoke. We sat on milk crates in the shaded alleyway. She lit. I just breathed the usual city air, already on fire in the heat.

"The bakers arrived last night to start shift & found a tree growing up through the sink drain. A few tiles had popped."

"Oh. What kind of tree?"

"They didn't say. They cut it out." She exhaled smoke. "Bacch, I can't see you anymore."

"You wrote *fuck you* on my mirror."

"I don't even remember why we fought." She looked at the brick wall.

"You've met someone & you're trying to push me away?"

"It was fun, really."

"The fight? Or me?"

"All of it, really ..."

We used to experiment together, grooving in a living room shared with friends, massaging each other, smoking & having deep & meaningfuls & sometimes chomping on watermelon because we couldn't swallow anything else. It can open you up to other people, to yourself, to your surrounds, to your senses, with the rush of a river.

We kissed farewell in the alley among the milk crates. She tasted like old cigarettes & fresh bread. We almost got carried away, but back to work. I went home with a free loaf. The universe taketh & giveth.

I need a job.

My heart rejected yet craved Bianca at the same time. How is that even possible? Defences up at the slightest stirrings of emotional depth. We were unstable to the point of exploding with food fights & fucking on floors. She was gone now.

More inspections that arvo. The place was clean, but still not much interest. A girl called Cicely came by. She liked the balcony, and my wine collection. I don't know why. I only had a 'collection' because there was a dozen-bottle discount at the shop. I'd already drunk five. Nothing was older than three years. I offered her a glass. It's important to get to know potential housemates, to know if they'll send you insane or not.

We sat on the balcony, drinking, watching the trains come & go, skyscrapers bending & sagging in the heat. Protests spilled out from George Street towards the station & Belmore Park. Protest organisers have to apply for permits from the Protectors, but they are never approved. People do it anyway. Unemployment is so high that there are always those with free time. Often, they're protesting Protector brutality. Protectors respond with brutality. We kept drinking.

"You don't have a TV," Cicely said. She was a recent graduate, bright-eyed, bony, halfway bohemian.

"Everyone has a TV in their pockets," I said.

"Anyway," continued Cicely, "all I see is terrorism & The Org on TV."

"I'd prefer to listen to music." I poured some more.

"And now they're gonna give terrorists the death penalty here. I wonder if it will be by injection, or hanging, or electric chair?"

I kept drinking. "How would you pay for this place?"

"I work for Media Ochre, with some photography on the side."

"You enjoy working for the MO empire?"

"Sure. In this age of misinformation & unreliable facts, we need at least one media source we can trust." She sipped & looked out at the city. "News shouldn't be a political spectrum. It should be truth."

"But can you trust The Org's truth?" I asked.

"Are you not a patriot? Why would you not trust The Org? The King?"

I sighed & drank. "Photography, ay. I need a professional headshot. Job applications, socials ... I could pay with wine?"

She left. I looked up graduate jobs. The prospect of doing any of them depressed me.

I must be broken.

Cristina

Inspections had not gone well. I visited a $600-a-week room that could barely fit a bed.

"Cozy!" the agent said.

Another place, $730-a-week, looked out on another apartment a few feet away, with a mural of the beach painted on it.

"Ocean views!" the agent said.

Another place, $720-a-week, was completely flooded. Water spilled down the front stoop when we opened the door.

"Indoor swimming pool!" the agent said.

The last place, in Glebe, was not through an agent but through an app, the way I'd found Bacch's in Surry Hills. I walked into the thin terrace living room past built-in bookshelves, bare other than some decorative sculptures and a chunky white Bible. The girl who lived there, Krystal, made some tea and we chatted in the kitchen. I admired her skin as she poured, her hair shimmering in the sunrays through the window, her neck, her lips ...

"So, what are you doing in Sydney?" she asked.

I swallowed, and sipped. "Um, I moved here to work for The Org. The Youth Program."

"Oh, delightful!" she said. "But why wouldn't you live at the dorms? My friend lives and works there with the Program. It's one big happy family, she says."

"I thought it might be a bit too much," I replied.

"How can you ever get enough of The Org? If you work there, you should be entirely dedicated or not at all."

"I just felt it might be ... restrictive. A bubble. I think I'm looking for more freedom."

"But they're fighting for freedom," she told me. "Freedom from evil and terrorism and drugs and spiritual disintegration. That's what the King says."

I noticed an extensive rack of wine and gin behind her.

"Yes," I said. "I agree. But what of personal responsibility, of choice?"

"You have no faith in The Org."

"You have no faith in people," I said.

"Believe whatever you want," she shrugged. "So long as it aligns with the beliefs of The Org."

We sipped tea in silence for a few moments. Her lips didn't seem so appealing, I told myself.

"Did you used to have more books?" I asked. "The shelves back there ..."

"The books belonged to the person who moved out. The Org has them now."

"The Org has the books? Or the person?"

"I'm ... not sure." Krystal took out her phone. "Hey, have you ever attended one of the King's rallies?"

"He doesn't travel to the country very often," I said, sipping the tea.

As much as I loved The Org, I was not fond of the King. His public speaking skills were the least of it. He was infamous, here and around the world, for attending summits and sexually harassing other heads of state, mostly the female presidents, but sometimes the men, too, even in front of cameras, on stages. Everyone knew. Many people hated him for that. He didn't care. Many people loved him for that. The Org was good at damage control, and diplomatic immunity meant he could never be prosecuted. But it had happened so often, and been denounced so many times, that several presidents, three queens, two prime ministers and one military coup leader were all beginning to threaten invasion. The King still didn't care, as Krystal was now showing me on her phone.

"This was me at his last one. See? I'll turn the volume up."

"First, they, they threatened sanctions," said the King, his voice tinny through the phone. "Now, they want to ... invade our country ... the Party even ... threatened to set up their own cities and ... settlements!"

The people at the rally were all screaming and waving Australian flags, the Union Jack flying with pride.

"Speak their own language and ... strip us of our own!"

The King raised his hand, holding a huge white Bible.

"They want to stop us practising our faith! Can you imagine? Can you even ... They threatened to breed us out! Take our children from us! Strip them ... children ... of their Australian culture! Their memories of where they grew up ... of family ... of love ... Can you imagine? We will not tolerate it. We are a strong nation. But we need to be stronger. Protector and defence spending is ... going to increase, and, and the citizen surveillance laws ..."

But by then, the crowd was too frenzied to hear the rest of it, their screams too loud for the phone to catch the rest. The video ended.

"That was ... wonderful," I said, standing up. "Well, thank you for the tea."

As I left, I couldn't help but glance at the empty bookshelf, the white Bible. The Org appeared in my mind, the building itself, my workplace, a monolith of offices among the Barangaroo high-rises, rows of IV trees lining the entranceways. Similar to the Federal Protectors building over on Goulburn Street, but even bigger. Skyscrapers are incredible. I still don't understand how people can make things so huge and beautiful. And want to destroy them.

After my induction week, The Org placed me in the sector that helps people with their gambling issues. Making a positive difference. My supervisor, Mr Ogglesworth, showed me around. He was middle-aged and wore suspenders. Big toothy grin.

"It's mostly paperwork," he said, "but soon you'll step up to work the support hotlines, if you don't get transferred to another sector. Find where you fit."

We walked beneath the low ceiling, all grey panels and air ducts and white fluorescent light tubes. Mr Ogglesworth continued the tour, emphasising his appreciation for filing skills.

"Administrative excellence is key to keeping The Org running like *cluckwork*."

"Did you say clockwork?" I asked.

"No. I said *cluckwork*, just like we're all chickens in the barn, doing our part for the farm. Any questions so far?"

"What do you think of The Org's new capital punishment laws?" I asked.

He stopped and turned to me, thumbs hooked into his suspender straps.

"Look, Cristina. Here, we don't concern ourselves with all that. But, between you and me ..." He bent forward, peering at me in earnest. "To protect the farm, to protect your animals ... well, sometimes you need to shoot some beasts."

I wondered how many farms Mr Ogglesworth had ever worked on, my soft-skinned supervisor of administrative excellence. But I didn't ask anything else.

The underground train back to Potts Point stank of hot sweat. Squished in with everyone, I found myself thinking of Bacch. The apartment. The view. The city. The giant screens shimmering with ever-changing adverts, so unlike anything we see back home.

Bacch didn't seem like he'd question me all the time, at least.

I wondered what he would think of my job at The Org.

Bacch

Fuck The Org. Now they wanted to outlaw sugar due to its health implications & potential for abusive consumption, as if we weren't already dying.

Cicely called to say she'd found another apartment to live in, had to move in asap. We hung up. I considered calling Bianca but decided against it.

A new boy inspected the place, but found somewhere better later that day. I looked for some jobs, drank some coffee with whiskey, and went to my tutoring session.

Everyone has a unique way of understanding the world. Finding how to speak to a person's attitude, their whole view on how they value education & life & themselves, that's how to teach, I think. Inspiration & vision. It seems to work. My dad was a teacher, but I learnt these things without him. In spite of him.

That arvo was a couple of high-schoolers in Randwick, in a red brick apartment complex. The young brother, Kafi, and the sister, Ria, lived with their parents & a grandmother. They ran a pretty successful sweets bakery nearby. Not the same as Bianca's. Ria and Kafi helped out, on top of their studies. Their mum always fed me creamy tea, and more donuts. I wondered what the sugar ban would do to them.

Ria & Kafi were first generation Australians, parents having fled here, copping years in offshore immigration detention on the way. We never really talked about it, though. Their parents still weren't confident with English, so I was there to support across their studies. I was pretty cheap. Ria would often stay quiet & reserved for ages until launching into a torrent of thoughts and insights, as if she bottled up her words, her voice, until she overflowed. Sometimes Kafi slept through our sessions, but otherwise he wanted to learn about everything he wasn't allowed to know or do. They were restless to explore the world, in their own ways.

"I just wanna drink goon at the beach one night," said Kafi that day, "and watch the sunrise in the morning, kissing a girl the whole time. That would be siiiiiick, bro. That's something to believe in."

Ria just read while Kafi continued. "Hey, bro, I have way too much body hair. It's gross, bro. I go to the beach with school friends & the girls & it's so embarrassing. Should I get waxed, bro? Should I?"

"Confidence," I said. "It's all you need. Own yourself, no one else."

"Brooo ..."

"Confidence is just a trick you have to play on yourself," I said.

"Do you fall for the trick?"

"Most days."

"Ugh," said Ria, without looking up from her pages. "Don't worry about your body hair."

"How can you not?" said Kafi.

Ria sighed, still reading, speaking quickly. "Your body is a weapon in the war of life. It's your choice whether you let others use it against you, or whether you wield it for your benefit. People will tease us anyway. But they're wrong. Colonists thought body hair meant you were like an animal, less civilised, less evolved. Easier to demonise & oppress people whose country you wanna invade & steal from. Why do we shave our body hair? Why should women be hairless? Like the school chaplain says, it's all 'being clean of sin'. To get some version of purity, of 'civility'. What is pure, anyway? It's so silly. I mean, people are still afraid of thinking of themselves as close to animals, close to nature, as if that's bad, instead of embracing what it truly means to be human."

"Um ..." I said. "Where'd you learn all that?"

"Obviously not from you, Bacch," laughed Kafi.

"Socials," said Ria. "Anyway, look. Can we actually do something here? You remember my history essay, on the early explorers, and mine was William Dampier?"

"Sure, the one who drew up all the botany records."

"Yeah. So, I added in those … extra notes we found."

I gulped. "And … how did your essay go, with those inclusions?"

"My teacher said I have to rewrite it, or else I'll fail."

"I told you it might be risky."

"But I had to try."

I sighed, thinking of my dad, proofreading my homework as a child, weeding out anything that didn't conform to the curriculum.

"I'm not going to rewrite it," she said.

"Why not?"

"Well … It's important that history is true, isn't it? That we can trust it? This Dampier guy, with all these places named after him, he's known as an explorer who first documented plants across Australia, but he also managed slave plantations in Jamaica, took slaves back to England. He was a pirate who raided settlements and fleets. Some said he was a cannibal. That's hectic. He was found guilty for cruelty against his own men. He called First Australians nothing but miserable brutes in his writings. He recorded the first English recipe for guacamole. He died in debt."

She threw her hands up. "How can I only include the botany and the guac?"

"What do you think, Kafi?" I said. "Even if it's not the whole picture, can you still be true, by selecting a few true things?"

But Kafi had put his head on his papers, and only mumbled a response.

"Look, Ria," I said. "I'm going to sound like my dad here, but you're smart. I had to make this decision too, every day. Do I want to graduate with good marks & career opportunities? Or do I want to fail, repeat years, struggle after school with no certificate, no ability to get into uni or a job?"

"But ..." she said, finally looking me in the eyes. "It shouldn't have to be like this."

"I know. I know."

I needed to piss, and excused myself to the bathroom. My phone rang mid-stream. I checked the screen. *Cristina Cute Housemate*. Oh. I answered.

"Hi Cristina."

"Hi Bacch. Is ... is this a bad time?"

"No, all good."

"It sounds like you're in the bathroom."

"I am."

"Right. Um, so, I'd like to meet you again. That is, if your room is still available?"

"Oh! Are you ... sure you'd like to live with me?"

"No."

"Ah."

"Hence asking for another meeting, to make sure."

"Ah."

We arranged a place & time to meet that night in Surry Hills. I flushed & washed & returned to the living space.

"Well," I said to Ria, huddled around the table. Kafi was asleep on his papers. The sink overflowed with dishes & cutlery & sweets & cakes.

"Well?" she said.

"Let's get that A+."

Cristina

I visited a Sydney bar for the first time. Approaching, I smiled at the huge security guard. His lips parted. His cheek twitched. Almost a smile. I continued to walk inside but he moved in front of me.

"ID."

I showed him. He looked me up and down, and walked over to a machine with a screen and a webcam thing that was looking at me.

"A little to the left, thanks."

"What?"

"Gotta scan your ID and take your photo."

"Why?"

"The Org will fine us otherwise."

"Oh ... Any other reason?"

"It stops alcohol-fuelled violence."

"Do you think so?"

He grunted and returned my license. "Enjoy your evening, ma'am."

Bacch was already seated at the bar when I arrived. He wore a light denim collared shirt, sleeves unravelled to the wrist, slightly too big for him. Black jeans, scuffed black shoes, hair dangling around his face.

"You look like you've had more sleep this time," I said when I reached him.

His eyes grabbed mine with a smile. Two drinks were on the bar. They were green, and on fire.

"What are they?" I asked, peering closely.

"Absinthe," said Bacch. "I just lit the sugar and plonked it in now. Shall we toast?"

"It's alcoholic?"

"Yes ..."

I stepped back. "I don't drink."

"Oh, why not?"

"Because it's bad for your body and soul."

"Do you eat ice-cream?" he asked.

"Ice-cream isn't as bad," I said, sliding into a seat. "It's not intoxicating. And it can be good for the soul."

"Shall I order you an affogato instead, then?"

"What's an affo...gato?" I asked.

"Ice-cream and a coffee shot."

"Aren't they going to outlaw sugar?"

"I guess they've made us outlaws then."

I ordered a water. Bacch blew the flames from one of the green drinks and drank it all in one gulp.

Hmm. Quite the impression. Mum and Dad didn't allow me to attend many parties in high school, but I started around sixteen. Everyone was drinking and smoking. I would bring a few cans of lemonade. The dancing looked fun. My friends would get looser and freer as the night progressed, all for the first time in our little lives. I'd end up helping people as they vomited, or consoling Tashi or Sami or Jordi when the boys they were kissing ended up kissing someone else, Tashi or Sami or Jordi or anyone really, so they'd dance with another and they'd kiss and they'd come back to me not knowing who was with who or if they really mattered to anyone.

"You matter to me," I'd said once to Jordi.

She leaned in to kiss me. I moved back, startled, and she apologised and lit a cigarette and muttered something. I leaned back in to hear her, and she turned to me, and everything slowed down as my heartbeat sped up, and our mouths fell into each other. I let it happen. It was my first kiss. She tasted like goon and ciggies. Her lips knew how to lead my lips, and tongues, and we pressed our bodies harder up against each other

26

for a while in the dark until her cigarette fell and burned my pants. We separated. She went off to dance and hook up and I went home soon after. Jordi never brought it up. I'm not sure she could remember it. I remembered.

"I mean how are they gonna ban sugar?" said Bacch, bringing me back to the bar. "They know it grows naturally in fruits, right? Anyone can grow it in their backyard."

"Well," I said. "I guess they'd have to go door-to-door, inspecting."

"Surely not."

"Or, back home, just before I left, The Org started a 'neighbourhood watch' program – basically dob in your friends, your family even, or risk being accused yourself."

"For what?"

"Anything."

"Wow," said Bacch. "Where was this?"

"A bunch of small towns."

"So, you're a regional girl, Cristi?"

"My name is Cristina," I said. "Please call me Cristina. And I ... I'm in the city, now."

"No worries, Cristina. Respect and open communication. The cornerstones of sharing space."

"I'm just worried about any bad habits you may have."

"All my habits are good habits." He blew out the flames on the second glass of absinthe. "Look, Cristi, Cristina, let's say we're both on trial for each other. You can bring in some plants of your own."

"I just need somewhere affordable. How can anyone afford this city?"

"Sorry guys," interrupted the bartender. "Last call. We're about to close."

"It's only eight o'clock?" said Bacch.

"New laws. We can't serve past eight anymore."

"What?"

"I know," said the bartender. "Soon they'll bring back the six o'clock swill."

"What's that?" I asked.

"For, like, half of last century," said the bartender, "bars had to close at six o'clock, so everyone would binge drink for an hour after work, on empty stomachs, before heading home for dinner with the family. The Australian way, all because of the law."

"Is there anywhere else we can go?" asked Bacch.

"The casino, bro. Or a licensed non-smoking restaurant."

Bacch opened his mouth to say something but stopped himself. We cheers'd; he finished his absinthe, I my water. We were near the apartment, so we walked there. I wanted a second look, with no icing on the carpet.

We walked up Elizabeth Street, a namesake of Queen Elizabeth, I guess. There was a woman sitting on the ground between the bottle shop and Woolworths supermarket, surrounded by several Protectors. I wondered what she was doing wrong.

"Yes," said one Protector, "but you need a permit to beg here."

"I need a fuckin *what*?" she said back.

"You need a permit," said another.

Bacch slowed his pace right down. I wanted to continue. I don't like to intrude on other people's trouble. The Protectors seemed even stricter here than back home.

"I'm just sittin, existin," said the woman.

A Protector kicked the lidless plastic container in front of her, rattling its contents. "What's that then?"

She grabbed at the container. "My fuckin *wallet*, mate."

Another Protector bent down and peered at her through his black visor. "You need a permit to beg. If you don't have one, we have to confiscate your donations, and ask you to peacefully move on. If you are unable to comply, we'll arrest you. This is your choice."

"Bacch," I said, a little further along the street. He'd stopped to watch while everyone else walked along minding their own business. "Come on!"

Bacch asked the Protectors, "Since when do you need a permit to beg?"

They turned to him. "It's the law, son. We're just enforcing the law. Move along, now."

They stood like a wall in front of Bacch, blocking the lady on the ground. He joined me but still stood watching. The Protectors confiscated the coins, counted them meticulously, over and over, placed them in a black bag, wrote some things down, handed the woman a ticket, and walked on. I wanted to give her some money, but then I could be breaking the law. Or she might be, again. I chose not to move.

Then she started screaming at the backs of the Protectors. But it was not English. It was something unfamiliar. The tones and syllables captivated me, if not for the heartbreak they conveyed. I knew nothing of the words. Nothing of the language. It didn't sound anything like those of the hostel.

Oh.

School only ever mentioned the lost languages of Australia. We were forbidden from ever learning or speaking them.

Passers-by passed by. Most had earphones in, perhaps not hearing a single thing. If they could hear it, they chose not to do anything.

When the Protectors heard her language, they stopped and came back.

"Bacch, seriously. Let's go."

The Protectors pulled the woman up and smacked her face into the wall as they cuffed her. Bacch stepped forward. A Protector approached him.

"No!" I called out.

"Can I help you, son?" said the Protector. "Are you trying to obstruct justice?"

Bacch spat on the ground.

The Protector grabbed him and threw him against the wall, too.

"NO!" I ran to them. "*What are you doing?*"

"Your friend spat at me," said the Protector.

"Look, sir," I pleaded. "We're just trying to go home."

"He's not going home."

"Please!" I screamed. "I ... I work for The Org."

"Well, you're too young to be a Servant."

"I'm almost finished the Program."

He lessened the pressure against Bacch.

"Please, he's ... not well, mentally ... and physically ... bad sinus issue. His disrespect for your authority was just ... just a natural, bodily function. I take care of him."

"You need to do a better job," said the Protector. He let go of Bacch. "Now, son, do you understand that what you did was gravely wrong?"

A few other Protectors were standing around, watching.

"Son?"

Bacch straightened up to look at him through the visor.

"I asked you a question, son. Do you understand that you are in the wrong?"

"Yes."

"Yes?"

"Yes, sir."

"We're going to let you go with your carer from The Org." The Protector stiffened. You could hear the uniform crackle. "Say 'thank you.'"

"Thank you."

"Sir?"

"Yes?"

"No, no, you're not the sir. I am."

"Ok. Sir."

"Now say, 'Thank you, sir.'"

"Thank you, sir."

"Finally. Fucking idiot."

The Protectors walked off. The woman had already been taken away. I couldn't hear her voice, her language. Disappeared from the land, save for some blood on brick.

I was in shock. Bacch and I looked at each other. His forehead was cut.

We walked home.

Bacch

Kindness costs nothing. If only booze & weed & life cost as much.

Cristina & I walked home in silence, until I had to ask her:

"Do you really work for The Org?"

"No." She didn't look at me.

"I didn't figure you for a liar."

"What?"

"With the Protectors, I mean."

She stayed quiet the rest of the way. We reached the apartment building & entered, climbing the stairs.

"Where do you work, then?" I asked her.

"I ... help people with gambling addictions."

"It's so odd, isn't it," I said.

"What? You don't believe me?"

"No, your job is great. But gambling addiction. We get told that it's the chemicals in drugs that get you hooked, get you addicted, and down you go from there. But you don't take anything with gambling. You don't smoke or snort or drink it. Same with social media addiction, or shopping addiction. And not everyone who tries drugs, alcohol, or gambling gets addicted to it. So, addiction can't only be about the substance, it must be something specific in the person, in their circumstances."

"Like, a moral failing?" asked Cristina.

"Um ... no ..."

We passed a fellow tenant, Jeffrey, as he left his apartment. He had wild hair, and a nose that had seen some fights.

"Oh! Hi Bacch," he said, stepping aside for us to pass. "Say, got any of those finger buns on you, mate? Lamingtons? I'm absolutely *stingin* for some of that sugary bread, y'know?"

I could almost see the saliva foaming in the corners of his mouth.

"Sorry Jeffrey, my bakery contact has dried up. I hear they're cracking down on society's sugar intake."

"Too bad, too bad … And your internet? Howzat?"

"Slow & sketchy, as always." I moved to keep walking, trying to showcase the place to Cristi, but Jeffrey was on for a chat.

"Yeah, yeah I'm thinkin I might sign up to The Org's network. It's the only way they'll ever get round to settin up the connection here properly, instead of this copper wire bullshit."

"I'm not sure how comfortable I'd be with that," I said.

"Yeah, me neither, me neither. But whaddaya do ay? Well, stay cool today …"

Jeffrey disappeared downstairs. Cristina & I continued up until we reached my front door, wide open, tunes banging from my stereo. We walked in. It was Hari. He was dancing around the living room with no shirt on, smoking a joint.

"Hari! How did you get in?"

"I never gave back your spare key. Hee hee."

"C'mon, to the balcony."

I took a seat out there. We had no lawn up there, no grass, but there were some old astroturf mats, fraying at the seams. Cristina went to the kitchen to grab a damp cloth on her way. Outside, she wiped some of the blood off my forehead. Her fingers touched my face with gentle care, but she scrubbed the cloth hard.

"Whaaaaat happened to you?" said Hari, peering through his locks.

Hari was a Filipino Aussie, a musical cratedigger, an absolute madman. He had black curly hair that hung around his gorgeous smile. We'd almost slept together on a few occasions, years back. Always wondered.

"Protectors hit me," I said. "Hari, please meet Cristina. She helped me. She might be my new housemate."

"G'day Cristina." Hari held out his hand. "Was he stirring shit again?"

"He spat at a Protector," said Cristina, wiping off the last red streak.

"Bacch, that is the dumbest shit I've heard today."

"They're getting worse," I said. "More aggressive."

"Wanna drink?" He gave me the joint & walked inside. I offered it to Cristina. She refused. The music changed a few times. Hari called out.

"Are you listening to this? This guy is from Germany, originally a houseless percussionist on the streets of Berlin, fuckin *genius* ... Oh man, you gotta listen to these fellas, they're from a farm town outside Bandar Abbas in Iran, but they moved to Detroit to make dirty sex-house tunes before Trump revoked their visas ... *geniuses* man, fuckin *geniuses* ... Shit are you listening to this? From Brazil, became a samba-bop-stab-phunk producer after doing peyote in the Amazon during the last pandemic & now he's pioneering the sound in Rio ... *fuckin GENIUS –* "

"Is he crazy?" asked Cristina.

I laughed. "Do you like this kind of music?"

She scrunched her nose. "I can see why people like it. It's too repetitive for me, but it flows nicely."

Hari returned with three beers, offered them around.

"Thanks, Hari," said Cristina, "but I don't drink."

Hari & I shared the unwanted bottle. A scattered glow of street lamps & office lights lay before us, as the veil of night fell across the city.

"How is your mum, Hari?" I asked.

"Not good," he said. "She could drop any minute. But, couldn't we all?"

"How's work?"

"The DJing is definitely drying up. Venues have to cut back their hours with each new law. So I downloaded this app, to sell myself, you know, ay. Sex work is work. Everyone prostitutes themselves in some way. Even started getting clients at The Org. You know what they use the prayer rooms for at The Org? Ay?"

Cristina moved as if to say something, but didn't. She looked out at the sprawling city. I couldn't figure out the expression on her face. Hari just smiled & absently took out his phone. We drank & smoked some more.

"Hari," I said. "We'll need those keys back."

"Have you heard?" he responded, looking down at his screen. Electronic effervescence paled his face & popped his eyes like theatre make-up. "There's a report that some refugees in off-shore detention have been waiting over a decade for their asylum applications to be processed. Ten years! They're sewing their mouths shut, literally sewing their lips, hundreds of humans on hunger strike. A few have died. Others ... it says others have escaped *back* to their countries to risk death. 'At least the firing squad is quick', said one. 'Australia tortures for years.' Damn. I'm glad they have the emoji options. I wouldn't want people to think I actually 'like' the content of that article."

The digital sound effect plinked out as Hari's thumb tapped his screen.

"Frowny face. There we go. So! We getting fucked up tonight or what?"

"Does that news not outrage you?" said Cristina.

"The article? Sure. It's absolutely fucked up. Hence the frowny face." Hari finished off his bottle. "Hey, I went to McDonald's for breakfast this arvo & couldn't even get served because a fucking venus fly trap had grown out of the floor in the children's playground area, right where the Hamburglar slippery dip spits you out at the bottom, and yeah they had to shut it all down. $32 avocado on toast at the café next door though. So reasonable. Until twelve fuckin Protectors came through the café with a dog, strip searched all the staff while people waited for coffees. Oi there's a warehouse party on tonight in Leichhardt. Should be siiiiiiiiick."

"Are you ... high?" asked Cristina.

"Ha!" he screamed. "Yes, yes I am & I don't care who knows it!"

"You seem very energetic," she said, eyeing him.

"That's because it's a sativa-dominant strain of cannabis. And I'm an energetic human."

"I didn't know there were different ... strains."

"Well," said Hari, leaning against the railing, smoking, smiling up there in the city sky. "Most of us in the land of Aus think there's only two types of buds, ay – bush & hydro. The classics. Get the Gatorade bottle & hosepipe brudda. But there are different strains, effects, terpenes, levels of CBD & THC, all of which we have natural receptors for, plus the pure landraces, the indica to the sativa – even proper glass billies. Who is anyone to tell you how you're allowed to regulate your own body & mind?"

"He's a nerd for it," I said, sipping.

"A nerd who does drugs?" said Cristi. The wind touched her hair in the late evening air. The clouds behind her drifted from soft orange to soft purple.

"Of course," he said. "Curiosity is motivation. Isn't it fascinating that our feelings, our very *being*, are a result of neurochemistry? Of a natural flux & balance, somehow giving rise to consciousness? *Brain soup*, ingredients mixed up & fuckin *steaming*??"

"That's why it's dangerous to mess with," said Cristi.

"Yeah. And alcohol kills more than five thousand Australians every year," he said. "A hundred thousand Americans."

We were quiet for a while on the balcony. The city sounds seeped in around us.

"I also, ah ..."

Cristi & I looked at Hari as he gazed out. He swallowed & rubbed his chest before continuing.

"My cousin stopped breathing last weekend. I had to do compressions & the breathing thing for like twenty minutes. My arm still hurts. The woman on the emergency line talked me & her friends through it, wish I could thank her. Overdosed at her own birthday. Accidental, but still ... Drinks, bags, pharmaceuticals, everything. Just, not breathing. We had to keep her lungs ... her lungs working."

"Is she ok?" I asked, shocked by the heavy turn. "Are you ok?"

"She was out of hospital next day. We'll be fine. Sorry to drop that one on you, Cristina. But yeah. Life is dangerous ... Another drink, anyone?"

He went inside.

I looked at Cristi – Cristina – and apologised. The purple clouds were darkening to grey behind her.

"It's ok," she said. "But should he be partying & drinking & whatever else, after all that?"

"I guess it's how some people deal with things."

"Deal? Or cope?"

I took a deep breath, but we remained silent.

"Do you still want to move in?" I eventually asked.

Her eyes peered off the balcony. Night had fallen around us. The city lit up.

Sunsets happen too quickly.

"*Are you listening to this shit??*" called Hari from inside. "*FUCKING GENIUS...!!*"

Cristina

Bacch had chunks of old soap sitting on the shower shelf, like dead bleached coral from where the Great Barrier Reef used to be. I cleaned them out and bought a litre of body soap gel to share. A couple of cockroaches met their deaths beneath my shoe, stomped, dragged, crushed, and not without a fight. Giant, mutant things.

Something felt strange, my first nights in the apartment. I was still getting used to the city sounds. No morning chatter of galahs and rainbow lorikeets, no sunset laughter from kookaburras in the canopy. Here, like the hostel, was a cacophony of honks, sirens, beeps, screams. Another world, where life spilled out in a mess across concrete, and birds dared not venture.

Even the air didn't feel right. Too hot, yes, but something else too.

The sensation followed me to The Org for work, where in fact the air conditioning was always too *cold*, but no one seemed to know how to change the settings. Even the climate in the skybridge via Level 73 – the only place there's any greenery – seemed artificially, mysteriously maintained. My level was 19 – Gambling Support, same as the cafeteria, all stark silver and steel, like the trays they serve the food on.

I'd made my own food for the first time, in my new kitchen, so I went up to 73 to eat. The elevator was huge, with mirrors on all sides, causing your image to cascade in infinite replicated reflections. People said there were multiple elevators with different levels of access. No one seemed sure just how high The Org went. I walked out and along the vast skybridge, a giant long park reaching the rooftop of the adjacent Media Ochre building, stepping beneath dazzling green fronds and gargantuan flowers in constant bloom, all hooked up, all plugged in. I stepped off the path and sat in the grass near a palm tree, complete with its bulging sap veins and IV drip. I whispered a prayer and began to eat.

Still, no birds.

Around me were hedges crafted into all kinds of animals and patterns and post-post-post-modern sculptures. Migrant gardeners with face masks sweated in their long-sleeved safety shirts as they mulched colourful flowerbeds. Giant Chinese blossom trees towered several stories high, out over the skybridge, their branches in fiery bloom against the heat. The views of Sydney below were utterly breathtaking.

A boy and a girl approached from across the lawn. I recognised them from the inductions. We waved to each other. I tried to quickly chew and swallow my mouthful by the time they reached me. The boy had his hair slicked back, the sides and back cut razor short. He wore a white collared shirt that fit perfectly, black pants and polished shoes. His movements were skittish – too much coffee? The girl wore a tasselled white dress and a warm smile in spite of the slight gaps between her teeth. Long black hair, glasses. Asian, though I wasn't yet familiar enough with faces, or accents, or the world beyond me, to discern her background.

"Cristina, right?" said the girl.

I swallowed the last lil bit as I stood up to greet them.

"Sure. Wendy, is it?"

Wendy nodded. I caught myself looking at her neck, her exposed collarbone, for a little too long.

"Patrick," said the boy, smiling as he stepped closer. "May we join you for lunch?"

"Sure."

They sat down. They were eating from containers with chopsticks, all kinds of oily noodles and dangly strips of veggies hanging on for the ride between bowl and mouth. I had no idea how to use chopsticks. I kept on with my sandwich.

"You don't live at The Org dorms, do you?" asked Patrick, between mouthfuls.

"No."

"Sydney girl?" asked Wendy, food still in her mouth. "I didn't expect that, honestly."

"No ... I was just too late to apply. Where are you from?"

"Sydney too," said Wendy.

"No," I said. "I mean where are you *from*?"

Patrick chortled, but Wendy pursed her lips. The noodles stopped moving toward her mouth.

"Do I talk with a fuckin accent?" she said.

"No, no," I said. "I'm just interested in your –"

"I hate the Party. I love The Org. I'm a believer. Is that what you wanted to know?" Wendy sighed. Her shoulders fell, and her eyes left mine. "My parents escaped to come here."

"I'm ... sorry."

"Just don't 'other' me by default. Ignorance isn't an excuse to be thoughtless."

I was silent in agreement.

"Well," said Patrick, eyes darting between Wendy and me. "Which... which sector do you work for? I'm in Indigenous Affairs."

"Wait," I said. "I really am sorry. And I thought The Org *liked* the Party."

"No, they recently announced the opposite, that it had always been this way."

"Oh."

"You'd better keep track of who our allies are," said Patrick, "and our enemies, if you're gonna work at The Org."

I took a bite of my sandwich, eyeing him, chewing.

"I work for the Parking Fines and Road Tolls Sector," said Wendy, finally letting her noodles travel all the way to her mouth.

"I'm keen to climb the floors of The Org and become a Servant," said Patrick.

"Following in his father's footsteps," said Wendy. Patrick frowned.

"Don't you also want to help people?" I said. "To help The Org help people?"

"Oh, yeah. Sure."

"Of course."

They helped themselves to the last of their lunches before seeing some other dorm friends across the park. They called them over. I packed up my things and excused myself.

"You have to go?" asked Patrick, looking me up and down.

"It takes a while to get back down to Level 19."

You know when your voice disappears and your bones ache with melancholy and you don't want to face another human being? Social self-sabotage. A swift goodbye. I passed under giant cherry blossom branches, back inside the building.

Moving your life between hostels, apartments, a new city, a new job; I felt disjointed, untethered, full of fantastic, terrifying possibility. I did not feel like myself, whoever she was.

Bacch helped move my few bags into his place. *Our* place. We passed a Chinese grocer, full of packets and jars and brands and ingredients I'd never seen before. I thought of Wendy and realised how little I knew about anything.

I did buy a plant to care for, a frangipani pot for the balcony, like the wild bushes along the driveway back home. Mum always picked frangipani flowers to decorate the dinner table centrepiece. I started doing the same. Bacch encouraged me after I first did it.

He also said we should have a housewarming dinner on Friday, that I could invite whoever I liked. But there was no one else I wanted to invite.

Bacch

I was in a rush to the bottle shop. I'd read online that new closing hours had been legislated for bottle shops. I'd also read that it only applied to old city zone demarcations. But the Google listing hadn't been updated, and the shop wasn't answering the phone, so I ran downstairs & out the door & hit Elizabeth Street with speed. I had plenty of wine at home but special occasions warrant a more sophisticated drop, even if I'd be the only one to enjoy it on this lovely, sweaty Friday night.

I turned a corner & ran straight into someone running the opposite way. We teetered in the halted haze of confusion.

"Sorry!"

"Ria?"

She kept running, her satchel flying behind her, the same one I'd seen Kafi rest his head on during tutoring. Protectors ran past me, caught up with Ria, tackled her to the ground, cuffed her, screaming, and dragged her off around another street corner.

"Hey!" I called out to the Protectors. One approached me.

"Yes ... son?" He was panting hard.

"Why is she being arrested?"

"Resisting arrest."

"Why the arrest in the first place?"

"She was searched ..." [wheezing] "... she had blasphemous books, in a busy public place ..." [bent over now] "... books of different religions, not even agreeing with each other ..." [veins popping] "... Imagine the damage she might have caused ..." [sweating] "... ideologically, at least ..."

"But is that illegal?"

"That is ... for the courts to decide." He stood up straight, the physical agony shining from him. "Do you know that girl, son?"

"No, I ... no. I was just curious."

He heaved in a few more breaths of the city air. "Best to keep your curiosities to yourself, son. Loose lips sink ships. You never know who is listening through smartphones these days. Well, have a nice day, son."

He disappeared around the street corner in pursuit of the others.

I tried calling Ria's family, but no one answered.

Do you pick your battles, or do your battles pick you?

I ran, fearful for Ria, for myself, as if I too were running from the Protectors, guilty by association. Elizabeth Street was packed with sweating pedestrians not looking at anything or anyone. Pores seemed to open up even in the concrete & asphalt, perspiration & plant life seeping through. People would surely start slipping soon.

Well. The bottle shop was closed. A sign on the door blamed structural repairs due to rogue natural growth. A woman was sitting on the ground nearby, a takeaway container in front of her with some coins. She looked similar to the other, but was not the same. Reeds & lilies grew up around her, from cracks in the footpath. I wondered what her story was, but I made no effort to ask her. I had no coins to give. I hoped she had a permit.

Running back into the apartment building, sweating, Mrs Clancy from the ground floor asked if I had any cinnamon scrolls or damper loaves or lamingtons. I had none of those to give either.

Cristina

Bacch was late for dinner. He hadn't even started cooking yet. Probably off on some adventure within the few blocks down to the store. Always out, chasing something.

We rarely saw each other in the mornings. Well, sometimes I saw him stumble in delirium to the bathroom, rubbing his eyes or his crotch, wearing nothing.

He must sleep naked. It's so hot in my room I've considered the same. But why doesn't he cover up? He knows I'm here! Is that why he doesn't cover up?

He saw me looking once, half waved, full smile, and closed his bedroom door again behind him. I almost choked on my cereal. I couldn't bring myself to approach him about it. I didn't mind, really. It wasn't *such* a bad sight before work.

I was looking forward to dinner at home. Restaurants can be pleasant, with great food, or terrible food, chatter and clatter. Perhaps people like the distraction of the hustle and bustle. They need the noise. I don't. Is that what Bacch was seeking out there, constantly? His noise, his next fix of distraction? At least he kept his plants watered and the house somewhat in order.

The apartment was silent. Even the dull din of the city seemed too suppressed by heat to reach this high.

Perhaps I needed some noise, too. I put some music on the stereo from my phone. No electronic music, sorry Bacch. I stood in the middle of the living room, barefoot. The carpet felt luscious. My toes dug in. The guitar crooned. The urge to move stirred in my abdomen. My heartbeat quickened.

Sometimes I would sing in the shower, softly, before Bacch was awake. But I couldn't remember the last time I danced.

There was a gap in the music, a changeover. Hot silence. Clapton's cover of 'Cocaine' began. Of course, I wasn't exactly inclined toward the subject matter, but music transcends all that. Don't you think? It gives a glimpse into those worlds. My own adventurous insight into lives unknown.

My parents hated this song.

I felt my hips sway, knees bending in to the swing. My fingers clicked on every second beat. I closed my eyes and felt the carpet rise up through my feet, toes clenching and unclenching. Shoulders began to bob. Moved around the space. My head lolled from side to side, hair falling and flailing everywhere. My body hit every beat. Every note plucked me. Every caesura left my heart suspended, waiting to be dropped.

I spun and spun and sung and spun in that room. Nothing between me and the core of the earth. I didn't know if everything was going to be ok, but I was beyond that; I let go, saw the true spirit of things as they could be from behind closed eyes, dancing and flying and tripping and falling and *whoooooops –*

Bacch grabbed me under the shoulders before I hit the ground. I hadn't even heard him open the door, but there he was. He helped me upright. I turned to face him.

"Are you ok?" he asked.

I nodded. I was sweating, but so was he. More than me, even.

"Have you been crying?" he asked.

The music stopped. I wiped my eyes. We separated. We stood there, looking into each other's faces. Bacch's had changed since he'd been out. His breathing was all over the place. His face was taut, eyes heavy, distracted. No new bottle in hand.

"Did something happen?" I asked.

A new song began. It felt like an interruption of something. Bacch looked away. He shook his head and walked to the kitchenette to begin food prep. He uncorked a bottle of red he already had and poured one small glass, one huge glass. He passed the former to me. I didn't take it.

"Just to cheers," he said.

"Ok ..." I focused on aiming the glass and not smashing it.

Bacch shook his head. "Eye contact."

We looked at each other, again, and only gently touched our glasses.

This is not Holy Communion.

I sipped it with stage fright. Too much. I began to splutter. Red droplets hit the floor. A glass of water appeared and I grabbed it and drank, still coughing. Bacch placed his hand on my back, a gentle touch. He laughed a little. All of life was a joke to him. I didn't get it.

My body regained control of itself. "It's literally poison."

But I planted my hands on the counter's far end and pushed myself up to sit, legs dangling off the edge, while I sipped on wine and Bacch made tacos – which actually looked pretty easy, but I appreciated his efforts. He was cooking, after all, not me. I think it's all he knew how to make. Through the open windows, the city shimmered like a desert mirage. Clapton came on again. It all felt unknown, and good. Like I was playing a part I'd always wondered about but never thought I'd get to try.

"Tell me about where you're from," said Bacch.

"Well," I said. "It's a small town. A devout family."

"Did you enjoy growing up there?"

"I don't know ... Mum has never been in great health. Dad resents it, but he's caring. Religious. Like my older brother. He's training to be a Protector."

"Oh, your brother? A Protector?" said Bacch.

"Mm. Where did you grow up?"

"Ah, we moved around a bit," he said. "Bathurst, Byron, Betoota, Sydney, a few towns in between. We never finally settled. Mum was kinda untethered, except to Dad – and me. They were teachers. Dad was devout, too. Loyal to The Org's curriculum. I remember as a kid, I brought home a map of Australia, but instead of what we know, it had countless Indigenous nations, none of which were called Australia. Imagine, Australia not actually being Australia? But my Dad burnt the map in front of me, and reported the teacher. The Org sent Dad to a new school every few years, schools they identified as straying too far from the syllabus. We followed, of course. New schools, all the time."

Bacch's hands moved the knife through tomatoes and lettuce and onions with comfortable familiarity.

"He always brought this rusted bar fridge to each new rental, for the garage," he continued. "An old Kelvinator, covered in all these Org stickers, weird propaganda phrases, colours faded. A heavy ordeal to move it, every time. Dad would make me get his beers. The door stuck and needed a solid pull. The fridge was always chockas. I'd take one out and close the door. Sometimes it didn't shut properly. I'd pull it back, and see the shelves, completely full again, a new bottle in place of the one I'd taken. The thing hummed. It was the Magic Pudding of beer fridges. Even Mum started drinking. And Dad kept drinking."

Bacch kept drinking.

"My parents didn't do alcohol or anything," I said. "Except Mum and her prescriptions. They were both ... rather strict."

"In what way?"

I sipped. "Many ways."

"You don't have a purity ring on or anything."

"I ... I had a boyfriend back home. We ... did ... things ..."

"Aha." Bacch smiled, but it seemed gentle, only a hint of teasing.

I held the wine glass at my face, a shield.

"Do you have a girlfriend?" I asked.

"Not anymore. Remember the mirror you smeared?"

"That was her?" I chuckled, but wine stuck in my throat.

Bacch's eyes were tearing up, cutting the fresh onion. I passed him some paper towel.

47

It must be something specific in the person, in their circumstances ...

"Do you drink because of pain?" I asked.

"I drink because ... of pleasure."

The cutting board was wet with tomato juices. Strips of lettuce lay discarded among avocado halves and spice shakers and a knife covered in sour cream. The spiced mince and kidney beans cooked away on the stove, spitting out occasional golden oil droplets.

I imagined a spittoon spitting chewed tobacco back out at saloon bar patrons.

Ridiculous.

I imagined being at the saloon, sitting there, Bacch and another woman behind the bar, having sex right in front of me, in between orders, cocktails waiting to be shaken and poured, impatient patrons yelling, me climbing over the bar, joining in ...

I shook my head, amazed by the things God puts in our heads.

Do we really have free will?

"You were crying when you were dancing earlier," he said, not looking up from his preparations. "Why?"

I drank more wine. It was tasting better. I jumped down to start setting the table.

"How long were you watching me?" I eventually asked.

"Long enough to know you can move."

I was silent. I felt like a champagne bottle, ready to burst, corked too long in bubbly confines.

Dinner tasted wonderful. No choice but to eat with your hands. Things got messy. I couldn't stop laughing. Bacch was being cheeky. Nothing was beyond the apartment. I didn't think about The Org, at least for a little while. Conversation fluttered elsewhere, tickling us. We spoke of dreams and music and hope, avoiding the topics of rising seas, rising unemployment, terrorism, the refugee crisis, the housing crisis, pandemics, deforestation, floods, fires, everything unpleasant beyond our walls. Bacch had cooked enough for leftovers but we ate almost everything. My toes squeezed the carpet as we tore through the night together, up in our little apartment among countless other little apartments.

Later, on the balcony, Bacch smoked his marijuana while I drank chamomile tea.

Bacch

I was hungover. Again. More & more cracks were opening up along the walls & more & more little yellow wattle flowers were sprouting. The owners weren't going to fix it. They were going to destroy it.

They're going to evict us.

Two weeks notice was in everyone's mail slots downstairs, and in our emails – only to the listed tenant, not Cristina.

The Sunday after next, we had to be gone. I'd always known it was coming, but I had hoped for more time.

"I understand the need for development," I said to Hari on the phone. "The population exceeds infrastructure. Our city is under constant construction, chock-full, too many of us, invading our own personal space, a decaying cadaver, too many worms clambering over each other for a breath of rancid air, wheezing exhaust fumes from ventricles & pipes no longer in service, or superficially maintained, to the extent that the bastards can get away with it. Or so it seems. I may be wrong."

"Mate," said Hari. "Are you ... ok?"

"Just ... the shock." I sighed. "A world forever under construction. A soul forever knocked down & rebuilt. A city burying itself in its own rabble & rubble. Anyway ... How are you? How is your cousin?"

"Yeah, fine. Oi, come to this rave tonight," said Hari. "Church theme. Caps, some joints to ride the roll later on, and a few bottles of wine to share. Dress up."

"Ok."

Perhaps it really was time to leave. But Cristina had just moved in. We'd only just met, and we already had an expiry date. Two fuckin weeks.

I put on red skinny tracksuit pants, a red vest, no shirt, and a red leather choker with a metal clip. A demon, not a devil. I went to the corner of my bedroom, to the loose floorboard – the secret stash spot – rolled a j & took an Uber to a random place on Parramatta Road to meet Hari. He'd dressed as the actual devil, horns, short shorts and a red cape, his taut arms & torso on show. We walked a few blocks, talking shit, swallowing caps, swigging wine. It all hit pretty quick.

The rave was at a warehouse, small & dark & beautiful & ugly, a place of twisted refuge, absolutely thumping. Almost too hot for clothes, and a few actually discarded their flimsy outfits for a while, all drifting with the beat, faaark, repetition, the same old same old, out there & in here, but at least here you felt free for a lil while, graffiti everywhere. Hari knew a few people, all dressed in wild attire, robes & leather, smiling & grooving. They sold nangs at a makeshift bar for $9 a hit – another victim of inflation. Smoke machines & lasers. It was difficult to see most of the time.

With The Org regulations against music venues, this was our Saturday night alternative. Plenty get busted. You never know if the Protectors are going to find it. You really wanna get out of there if they show up.

Please, do not get caught by them.

Ria.

"The Org tried to outlaw clubs altogether," Hari was telling a few of us, shouting the words, his face flashing with coloured lasers in the moving darkness. "Like the UK in '94 with the ... I think it was the Criminal Justice & Public Order Act ... fuckin ... outlawing music performances – the official line was something like – 'wholly or predominantly characterised by the emission of repetitive beats' ... It spawned whole genres built on a non-repetitive beat structure."

"Ooft," said a girl in white robes & giant circle sunnies, bopping to the bass. "Just ... let us ... be, ay ..."

"Ay ..." said Hari, fist pumping to the beat. "Ay. Listen to that vocal. DJ Eddie Amador, 1997. Legend. Visionary. Classic shit."

Not everyone understands house music
It's a spiritual thing
A body thing
A soul thing

So, we grooved, sonic frequencies moving through us, like we were malleable, a substance constantly in motion, a city under construction, a universe expanding, and the succession of repetitive beats seeped in like water through soil, churning & digging up things we don't let grow or that aren't allowed to grow.

The bathroom upstairs was so filthy that I refused to take my pinga-poo in there. There was even a cactus patch growing out of the urinal. I couldn't hold on. I went outside & tried to find a bush or tree to shit beneath, but there were none in sight, just tarmac & paths & parking lot spaces around other warehouses. No grass. What could I do? Nature was calling, but the city couldn't answer.

I found a gutter & bent down, pants at the ankles, begging for a clean snap. The sky glowed orange from the night lights of Port Botany & the rest of the city, no stars peeking through the clouds to see me. I finished & returned, used someone's hand sanitiser. Later I couldn't find Hari because someone he'd just met was fucking him in the bathroom I'd thought too dirty to get dirty in.

I found myself sitting in a dark corner for a while, amongst people's jackets and bags, rolling from the cap, thinking of Bianca. Did I want her here? Did I want Cristina here? I closed my eyes, lights dancing across eyelids, remembering another rave, an abandoned brothel in Kensington, also owned by developers, soon to be torn down. The memory seemed so vivid. Rooms went off by themselves, some still with remnants of the building's past life, old shackles & X-rack set ups. They had no water or electricity, so they brought in generators, rigged everything up. The main room was filled with empty pools, as if modelled on an ancient Roman bathhouse of virile boasts & perverse secrecies. Well, when in Rome ... Hari found me in one of the side rooms, sitting naked on a couch chair against the wall, base-deep in an older guy's gullet, with Bianca kneeling on the couch either side of my head, riding my face, suffocating me, scratching at the walls as they vibrated with bass. The older guy was renowned for cock worship. He knelt at the altar, gagging on communion. I grabbed his hair as he sucked but it wasn't hair at all *it's a toupee my god* and –

I opened my eyes, hoping no one had heard me – but of course, I hadn't said any of this. Just paranoia. The Org outlawed homosexual acts for a long time, before changing the law back after a $525 million postal plebiscite that they said cost only $160 million. Looking back, if we were caught that night, I don't think Bianca could have been charged. For her, it was heterosexual, and The Org was still debating the semantics of a bill outlawing group sex at the time.

Sexuality is a slippery spectrum – not a sin.

My only way to defeat shame is to become shameless.

I stood up from the corner, shaking my head as I rolled through waves of horny introspection. I started dancing between bodies & priests & angels & demons & choir boys, trying to forget Bianca and the wild shit we always did. A gorgeous girl, as high as the stars on MDMA & ketamine, gap between her front teeth, started telling me how much she loved me, switching between languages to repeat it. She was dressed as a nun, habit & robe & white lingerie. I think she said her name was Winnie, or Wendy. We danced for some time. She wasn't great at it, but I liked her enthusiasm. Another track emerged from the mix that I recognised, a pulsing guitar lick with spoken word drifting throughout, Dino Lenny & Doorly. We all danced.

Well this is a story about a man that walks into this big, dark room
And this room is full of light
And full of smoke machines
And he feels like he is just - in his old house when he was a child
What it was like playing with his family
On his little bike
Feeling safe, and forgetting all his troubles
Forgetting what he needs to do
And who he has to be
And just not feeling inferior
There's no feeling inferior
In this room, worries and all the rules
What he can do and what he can't do, just vanish
The only thing that counts is respect
Respect your brother
And this room is a magic room
But it's really not about the room itself
It's about the people in the room
It's about the moments they share, the smiles
The looks, the music, the DJ
It makes you feel like you're one thing
It makes you wanna live forever
Instead of just thinking that it's you against the world
And you think, well why can't we all just live together like this?
Nothing is wrong
As long as we stay in the room
But when I walk out
I just feel I'm lost in the gloom

When you're in the high, the roll, time stretches on but, like many things that stretch, it snaps back to a size far smaller, and afterwards you realise that a night has passed in no time at all. Winnie left even sooner, with a smile & a wave. Hers was a careless love, thrown around, chemically encouraged, easily discarded. I was alone in a dwindling crowd of beautiful people.

A false sense of freedom had settled in. I was sure to be taught a lesson soon. No one can live so flippantly, with such joy, and get away with it.

Outside, waiting for the Uber home, I sat on the kerb of Parramatta Road. Hari lived in Marrickville and was waiting for his ride, smoking & looking off into the darkness.

"The remedy of eating new pussy on old MDMA just isn't cutting it," he announced. "The dread is closing in."

I nodded & smoked & wondered why we drive ourselves to do these things over & over again, night after night, day after day, office or warehouse, at work or at home. Imagine – Tracy Grimshaw grilling me grimly on *A Current Affair* over all my poisonous habits, destructive tendencies, too many shots of coffee, day after day, from unsustainable takeaway cups, how I'd lost all morals, all value to society, I was a disappointment to my parents, my country, my planet, a close-up of my neighbour yelling at me over the fence, as if I could ever afford a house with a fuckin lawn, viewers frothing.

The traffic lights flashed from red to green in the morning darkness. No cars. We sat there in the rare city stillness.

"Life is absurd, man," said Hari. "Everything is absurd."

I wondered if the King had ever been to a rave. Maybe then he'd understand.

I wondered what Bianca was doing. I wondered what Cristi was doing.

Every night should be taco night. Cristi laughed more than I'd ever heard her. She even danced a lil. Like flower petals opening up to the sun & sky. She shouldn't hide herself from the world so much, I thought.

Perhaps the world doesn't deserve her. I don't deserve her.

Heading home, alone, again, the car windows were slick with beads of leftover raindrops. They each reflected, in lil glowing droplets, all the lights of cars & buildings & street lamps & neon signs, so that Sydney flew by in blurred colours, wet, as if looking out through a glistening disco ball.

Cristina

It was Monday. I was at The Org, looking over the railing of the skybridge, lost in my daily lunchtime solitude. From there, you could see so much of the city. Nearby was one of the casinos in Barangaroo.

A shudder seemed to run through the gardenias and ferns near me. Like a shiver, over before you realise it happened. Yet there was no wind, even up there. I looked closer at the petals, the leaves. They were still.

Two distinct sounds seemed suddenly alive throughout the city, wrangling with each other. One was an overwhelming cosmic groan, low in register, massive in impact. I could feel that wrenching bass. The other was a piercing screech, like a sky blackened by screaming birds, like a tooth pulled without anaesthesia. They were the sounds of crunching metal.

I looked over the railing. The entire casino tower was leaning off-centre. Concrete catapulted through the air in pieces. All kinds of huge plants exploded out of the earth in a frenzy of pollination, breaking through the foundations of the building. Tree trunks escaped through glass windows, spraying broken shards everywhere. Giant vines like tentacles of mythological squids seemed to slide their grip up the building, squeezing with earth-shaking tenacity, bending crucial steel pylons.

I'd never seen a thing like it. It was as if the ground were swallowing the building in a flurry of jungle growth. Soon, Protectors were attacking the new forestation with chainsaws and flamethrowers. It all began to burn with immense flames. The rancid smell of burning oil and petrol stung my nostrils, and I had to look away to cough and wipe my eyes a few times. The Protectors did this instead of evacuating, burning it down while people still fled. The acrid smoke began to suffocate the building from the inside out. I could see people running from the ground floor outside to safety, shooting out from plumes of black, stumbling and struggling to breathe. The flames climbed higher. I didn't know what to do other than to just keep watching, until The Org alarm sounded for our own evacuation.

I ran back across the skybridge. Down the stairwell with everyone else, down to streets filled with orderly IV trees and human chaos. Men cried in coffee shops. Waitresses hugged their patrons for some semblance of comfort. Sirens and screams. I don't know why, but I ran towards the casino. The closer I got, the more evidence of nature's takeover appeared. It was as if the apex of a volcano had burst forth with an eruption of wild foliage. Roots slithered to take hold of the concrete. Protectors and emergency workers struggled to get through gnarled branches and giant palm frond thickets. People streamed out of the casino, some trampling others, many holding handfuls of singed cash and stashes of casino chips and phones with their cameras on to record everything, even their deaths.

Where was God to save us?

A crack burst through my senses, as if lightning had hit metres away. Something had exploded. A colossal burning tree smashed through the casino from the inside. Glass flew out in sharp shimmering pieces, catching reflections of firelight.

The Flaming Tree. The Voice of God before Moses.

But there was no voice. No commandments. No guidance. No lead. Just countless voices yelling over the top of one another.

Where were my mum and dad?

Protectors directed the onlookers to go home, and I allowed myself to be led away. I didn't know what else to do. I didn't understand. I was alone in the crowds.

Bacch

It was Monday. Thirteen days until eviction.

I opened the fridge. Cristina & I had separate shelves. Hers were chock-full with veggies & sauces & Tim Tams & milk & juice cartons. Mine had half a wrinkled lime, half a bottle of white, a few beers left by Hari & a beetroot tupperware container filled more with purple liquid than any actual beetroot. I threw out the lime, tasted the wine, threw out the wine, drank some of the beetroot juice, took one of Cristi's Tim Tams & closed the fridge. Phone was dead, so while it charged I left to buy a $19.99 Health Boost fruit juice before cooking up a mi goreng arvo breakfast, to be served straight from the stove pot held with tea towels because the handle broke off months prior, after a night spent drinking & indulging & celebrating & escaping life by trying to hide deeper within it, while accidentally breaking shit.

I never even got the fruit juice. The whole city was wild. Smoke obscured the sun. Screens towering above showed the burning destruction. Everyone was looking at each other's phones to see the news, all buzzing with alerts. I ran home & turned on my phone & tried & failed to get through to Cristi. From our balcony, I could see the huge column of smoke billowing up from the skyline, leaking out across the atmosphere above Sydney. I tried to distract myself with job applications & mi goreng.

Mum called. She'd seen the news. I assured her I was ok.

"Oh, I'm glad, honey, I'm so glad." You could always hear the silent gaps between sentences when she'd sip her wine. It was early arvo. "Such a sad event. How terrible."

"Very."

"The news also said there was a riot at a party, in the city." *Sip.* "You weren't there, were you honey?"

"Yeah, well no riot but the Protectors broke some ribs, smashed some furniture. Kicked a guy in the street."

"Were you ok?" she asked.

"Fine."

"Well … I'm sure they're just a few bad apples, you know. The Protectors are there to protect us."

"Mum, you know what the full saying is, yeah? *A few bad apples spoil the bunch.*"

"Yes, well …" *Sip.* "You know, Bacch, the grass is grey & brown up here."

"What?"

"The grass around the house, around town. The drought. It's all dead & dust, or on its way to it, you know. If we get fires, things will light up quick."

"Have they finished the new desal plant up there?"

"Nah. More delays." *Sip.* "But anyway … How's the job search going?"

"Fine. Still going."

"Smoking marijuana?"

"It's cannabis, Mum."

"Oh, I know, it's just what we always used to call it." *Sip.* "How about pills? Powders? Chemicals?"

"Um … no, Mum. Not too much."

"That's good. Oh, you'll find a job soon, son. Someone will see your potential."

"Does Dad wanna talk?"

"Oh, um, one sec."

…

…

...

"He said he's not here."

"Ok. Well, I love you, Mum."

"You too, darl. Please just stay safe out there." *Sip.* "The world is too dangerous."

I went back to pacing the living room, listening to calm tunes, unfolding the eviction notice & folding it back up, taking books from the shelves & reading a random page over & over again before pacing again for a while, before picking up the eviction notice again & again until I couldn't stand it & ran out the door & down the stairs, as someone called after me asking whether I had any cheese & bacon rolls to sell them cheap so they didn't have to risk leaving their house, until I burst through the downstairs foyer & out to the street & ran into Cristina as she ran into me, our arms grabbing each other in a rough embrace that spun us around, but we held each other.

Masses of multi-coloured human beings walked back & forth around us, all trying to find happiness somehow.

We held each other tight.

Cristina

I told Bacch what I'd seen. Words spilled out from me in an uneven, shaky flow. It was if hell had opened its gates to swallow us for our countless sins. Yet it was like a rainforest had erupted, too.

Is nature the devil? Are we the devil? Are we nature?

I felt guilty about such thoughts, without really knowing why.

Can The Org read minds?

At home, after I'd calmed down, showered, reset myself, we watched the news coverage on our phones.

The King only ever came out for rallies or big occasions, offering a voice, for the Org, for the people, a comfort. This was big enough. The King and a casino representative gave a press conference together in front of the towering pile of burning rubble. Two men with grey hair and dark blue suits, red ties, white shirts. You could tell them apart, at least, by the eyebrows.

"A senseless act of terrorism," said the rep.

"And due to ... to the swift action of the Protectors," said the King, "we already have the culprits in custody. The ... The ... The Casino Three."

He still wasn't a very good speaker, always took far too long in his gaps between words, as if he forgot what he was talking about at every utterance, forcing out every syllable.

"Indeed," said the rep.

"We don't know ... much about how they did it ... but we do know that they are all highly dangerous and hateful towards Australian values."

"Yes, quite," said the rep.

You could still see Protectors in the background, salvaging bodies and hacking at branches.

"We won't name them yet, because we don't know –" The King faltered. "I mean, for their privacy. But, they will be brought swiftly to justice, and executed ... publicly. Within the fortnight. It is for the greater good that our capital punishment laws have finally been amended ... so, so as to be ... consistent with the world we really live in ... WE are terrified and terrorised. THEY deserve the death penalty."

"Yes, quite," said the rep.

"We have lost many lives today ... We have also lost ... one of our city's greatest casinos."

"But, praise The Org, we have another one."

"Yes," said the King. "Now you understand the importance of always having more than you need. And, in fact, the surviving casino has, has a lunchtime schnitzel deal right now in the food court ... so head on down for a great meal and maybe a play on the pokies or a spin at the tables. Who knows? You might even ... *WIN BIG*!!"

"Enjoy that generous schnitty deal, folks," said the casino rep. "Support our troops and our Protectors! And follow us on social media."

"THEY deserve the death penalty!"

"God bless Australia!"

Cheers.

We flicked through more articles and videos. Commentators from all ends of politics were uploading footage of themselves seething, filling the entire screen with their faces and tongues and spit. Viewers were commenting on the commentators and sharing and getting riled up and seething too. Bacch showed me another video – on the *Q&A* television panel that night, Tony Jones had to mediate a physical fight between several people, shirts ripped and fists thrown. An all-out brawl erupted, panellists tossing each other across the huge table, spilling into the audience.

"I don't really know who Tony Jones is," I said, "but he sure knows how to bareknuckle."

I drank wine with Bacch again. Monday night. I wasn't beginning to like it, but life is messy. We lay on the couch together, snuggled up beneath a thin blanket. The heat still simmered, but we had the windows open, breeze blowing through, throwing our hair around, mine especially. Bacch fixed mine or I fixed his, a few fingertips sliding along his face or mine, tucking strands behind ears. No more screens. The outside world had had enough of us, and we'd had enough of it.

I went to bed and couldn't sleep and couldn't even pray.

I saw some people die today.

Bacch

Time marches on regardless of tragedies & happiness & life-changing incidents. Sydney mourned the loss of one of its most prized casinos. All unapproved vegetation was diced up; another aspect of nature now deemed illegal by The Org. Workers drove machines like clunky robot dinosaurs, roaming the city blocks, reaching out with steel arms, all claws & jaws, devouring & destroying every branch, every leaf. Cristi said she heard the sounds of monolithic chainsaws all day from her gambling support office.

Many were claiming that all of this growth throughout the city was actually an act of God, though no one could agree on whose God was responsible. Some claimed it was La Pachamama, Mother Nature, engaging her own revolution up through the concrete. But the proponents of such ideas were branded as dirty hippies, heathens, foreigners, communists, addicts & criminals, their homes raided, their property seized. It was difficult to discern what was real & what wasn't, with such speculation. Scientists asked to study the devastating phenomena, but all requests were rejected.

I finally visited Ria's family. Protectors had come only hours earlier with a search warrant, upturned the entire apartment. Dishes & pots & pans & sweets & jars & spice shakers were scattered everywhere. The living room was smashed up. The coffee table was in pieces, the TV facedown on the rug, surrounded by shards of glass. Ria's clothes & books & even all of Kafi's things had been thrown apart in their bedrooms.

We sat at the dining table. Their mother managed to make me some milk tea, as always, though her trembling hands spilled a good amount of it on the scuffed floor. Assorted sweets from their bakery were laid out.

"Ria is suspected of terrorism," said Kafi. "I dunno, bro ..."

I was out of my depth even as their tutor, let alone this. I wished Ria was there to say something wise. I helped clean up for a while before leaving. Walking to the bus stop, I passed their bakery. It was closed for the rest of the day.

Time marched on.

I spent the evening with Cristi at home, unplugged from everything except our own companionship. It wasn't the right time to mention the eviction.

When would be?

I looked around at nothing. Where was the optimism in the place? Our cultural insignia? What banner did we have to march beneath? What cause? The Org? The King? Were we so splintered & spread so thin? Where were our screams of dissent? Our outlaws? Driven to extinction, perhaps, culled from the evolutionary chain of humankind so that all we have left are predators & prey, forced to fuck each other over in the grand scramble for small legacies. And yet, we enjoy ourselves so much sometimes amid existence.

We drifted off on the couch together, Cristi & I, awaking in a haze, hours later, in the groggy night. Our bodies lingered. Then we each retired to our own beds.

Twelve days until eviction.

And time marched on.

Cristina

To perceive with the eyes of a traveller all things, as if for the first time, was the only way I knew how to survive the streets of Sydney, especially during those strange and sorrowful days. I'd never travelled much. The city was an unfamiliar beast.

How does a city breathe when the ground is so smothered? It steals back gasps through venues and shops and small energies of crawling humanity, bringing life to inanimate surrounds. People seemed to rush, trailed by hurried worries, while small secrets occurred all around them for the first and last time. Marvels of architecture rose up like shrines to engineering ingenuity, while splashes of teeming colours and hideaways of escapist offerings lined the streets. Even on my route to and from work at The Org, the same route every day, I always saw different faces, different outfits, different details, different moods, different differences to the life I once knew.

Everywhere I went, the red neon Westfield logo on top of Centrepoint Tower followed me around like the Eye of Sauron, visible everywhere. To get away from it, the inner city, sometimes I deliberately missed my stop coming home, or I'd jump off and jump on a random train on a random platform, slipping between the doors just as they closed. I lost myself in the sprawling Sydney suburbs. I'd find old terrace houses stacked wall to wall on quiet tree-lined streets, tucked away and covered in layers of fallen leaves, or barely finished apartment blocks that all looked the same, towering against sparse skies, with cranes nearby to construct the next block and the next. Sometimes there were hidden plazas with fairy lights strung up in trees around a fountain centrepiece, or streets of ornate restaurants and hookah lounges with cushions covering the floors. Multistorey walls played canvas to murals of dreamlike scenes and towering faces of all sorts, whose stares you could not avoid. I'd return to them later, just to see Protectors managing a cover-up job, workmen in high-vis in lift machines painting it all over with black. Of course, the next day there would be new murals performed with arching white spray paint, utilising the black background to create an entirely new story across the walls.

The striking thing about Sydney was how distinct certain areas were, shaped by different cultures and histories. I entered shops to ask questions, to observe places from the inside out rather than passing by, to engage somehow, to learn. But I was still a tourist. I did not understand the languages I heard, but I'd chat to people and smell the wafts of incense and massage oils and flaming charcoal and spices and even the occasional native flower that wasn't hooked up to IV drips, peeking through the cracks, and I'd feel hopeful that one day Australia could belong together, that the whole world could belong together.

We already could; we just don't all see it.

Bacch accompanied me to Bondi Beach. It was full of beautiful people walking ugly dogs. Not just dogs, in fact; sheep, possums, wombats, even the occasional octopus trailed slimy residue along Campbell Parade, their owners all sitting at cafés in colourful gym-wear doing hundred-dollar brunches with all these animals tied to fence posts. Young palm trees were growing everywhere, no IV drips attached, up through the boardwalk, making the ground uneven and difficult for prams and e-scooters. Protectors would take care of it soon enough.

I saw a group of young people and immediately thought they were one of the many dangerous African gangs The Org had been warning us about on the news; however, as I walked past, I realised they were just friends chatting around a table on a café terrace, laughing over frappés.

I liked exploring the city with Bacch. We didn't feel the need to talk all the time. Just being together was enough. We would laugh at what we heard in passing: chatter of corporate yoga retreats, vegetarian steaks, dream homes with multiple sports cars, mountain goat marathons, the true and inherent value of socials followers ...

We walked past some Amnesty International volunteers along the boardwalk, signed some of their petitions, continued walking to the beach. Some kids with skateboards watched videos of beheadings of enemy soldiers and journalist hostages on their iPhones, after an ad for a new iPhone. I needed to wash it all off in the ocean.

The beach was packed. Families, couples, elderly swimmers. A beautiful young woman was sunbathing topless. She looked European of some sort, though I can't say why I thought so. Perhaps the ruddy sunburn. I wondered if all the beaches in Europe were accommodating to nudity. We each stripped down, sun glancing from almost-untarnished skin, and went swimming on yet another summer day in Sydney. I didn't go gracefully, no feet gently immersing themselves. I attacked the waves. Bacch stayed in the shallows. I swam out far past the crowd.

The water was cold and I liked it. I dived under. And I screamed. Muffled by the sea, yelling. I came up for breath. Back down again. Scream. Up again. Breathe. Down again. Laughter, mad laughter, bubbling. No one could hear me. Perhaps some of the sea creatures below could hear, but *could they ever understand??*

Back on shore, the European girl had left. I thought about what Europe must be like as I dried myself off. Then Bacch and I walked to the bus stop to go home, talking of silly things that we'll never remember. We fell asleep on the couch together again that night. Our caresses were for comfort, but they betrayed something else, an excuse to feel each other, intimacy restrained. As we drifted off to the sounds of the stereo, as our bodies nestled into each other, Bacch's lips accidentally – or purposely? – brushed the back of my bare neck. It reached every organ inside me, for the slightest quivering moment.

Its echo lasted. My dreams were restless.

Bacch

Paradisiac Pty Ltd supplied fertility statues from the depths of Asia & Africa, love potions from Arabia, Aztecan avocados, entire banana trees swollen with fruit & grown in pots with IV drips, marble fountains gushing rich chocolate smuggled from Colombia, bushels of cherries genetically enhanced to explode with juice in your mouth as you bite in. All ordered through an app. Gotta do your research before a job interview. Well, internship.

Paid internship?

Wednesday. Eleven days until eviction. I needed a job. So far, I'd been attending interviews on time but at the wrong place, or at the right place at the wrong time.

Silly, hopeless boy.

So much potential, though …

Paradisiac was in the central business district. I sat, early, in a velvet chaise lounge in a reception area decorated with a chandelier hanging from the ceiling. I wore a suit, no tie. Cristi had tied one for me, standing behind me, very close, moving her hands with a flourish at my neck. But I'd spilled coffee on the tie while on the train.

The receptionist sat at his desk, glancing up at me every now & again from beneath gelled fluorescent hair, until the door to the director's office flew open.

Another young interviewee ran out past me, tie loose, hair roughed up, tears smothering his anguished face.

I hadn't quite processed this before I heard a woman summon, "Bacch," and then I was standing in the boss's office. The door closed behind me. She was sitting atop her desk, legs crossed from within a tight black business dress. Reading glasses.

"I'm Ms Bolt. Please, Bacch, take a seat. And some oysters." She motioned toward a plate laid out next to her on an ornate serving dish, two slices of lemon untouched, three already squeezed. I took a few oysters with thanks, knocked them back, and put them in the discards bowl beside the dish.

"Thank you, Ms Bolt." I sat down in the chair in front of her, also a velvet chaise.

"My pleasure. Something to wash it down?" She offered wine. I accepted. I could definitely see myself working here.

"What is this?" I asked, as she produced two glasses of rich red. "What are you doing?"

"Demonstrating our product line," she said with a sharp smile. She seemed in her mid-forties. We clinked & drank.

Knock knock at the door. The receptionist popped his head in, bright hair remaining perfectly in place.

"Ms Bolt, babes, the Servants are here to see you."

"Tell them I'm just finishing an interview."

The hair disappeared.

"Servants?" I asked. "From The Org?"

"A drop from the deepest cellar barrels beneath the Bradfield Manor of the Hunter Valley," she exclaimed, glass raised, eyes deep in the wine. "For generations, the Bradfields played host to all manner of aristocratic indulgences, secluded among their vineyards. Dinner parties for intellectuals, Australian & international politicians, writers & artists, these gatherings would blossom into orgiastic celebrations of life & love & flesh & grape, so much so that the ceaseless bacchanals seeped down into the cellars below. Ha, *Bacch*-anals. Well, the Bradfields were raided by The Org several years ago, of course, but that sultry magic nestled itself away in barrels & bottles sunk deep within the ground, away from the destruction of politics & Protectors. And now, here we are today to uncork & enjoy so many generations of human social experimentation & unrestrained lust, collected up in the pool from which we now sip."

"Jesus ..." I said, sipping.

"We're not at communion right now, Bacch."

"But do you really believe the story?" I asked, setting the empty glass next to the oysters & lemon slices. "All the aphrodisiac properties of your products? Or is it just ... bullshit?"

She raised her eyebrows & her glass. "It doesn't matter. It matters whether our buyers believe it. You don't seem seduced."

"I'm applying to be a seller, not a buyer, Ms Bolt."

She leaned forward, her bust wanting to leap out & punch me in the face. "And what is it that we are truly selling, Bacch?"

"Is this a test?"

"Yes. It's a fucking job interview. Answer the question."

"Well ..." I said, looking at the squeezed lemons. "The products are not what you sell. You sell inspiration, confidence, imagination, a sprinkle of magic upon otherwise normal things. These products have scant meaning unless people are convinced of their worth & effects. They'd rather be sold a fantasy. Or at least a distraction." I took another oyster & slurped it down. "Look, everyone has the capacity within themselves to feel strongly, in any way. We just lack that inspiration, that catalyst of passion, that belief in ourselves & in others."

"And what is your passion, Mr Bacch?"

"I ... I don't know."

"Lack of passion is fatal."

"Life is fatal, Ms Bolt."

She slapped me hard across the face.

"What the fuck?"

"I hate your kind," she said, lighting a cigar. "Bunch of narcissistic, entitled nihilists, all of you."

"I thought this had been going well."

"I just had to get that off my chest." She spat on the carpet next to me. "All the other young applicants come in here, telling me how much they believe in the products. They're either lying or fools. Create a charged atmosphere, a splash of animalistic energy, a hint, a flash, a suggestion, conscious or otherwise, with enough conviction that others are convinced. Everyone needs something to believe in."

She leapt from the table & began pacing the room. The window was open, but cigar smoke & heat still tickled my throat. She even lit an incense stick hidden in the corner.

"That previous fellow who ran out past you, sobbing, fell so fully & completely in love with me in twenty minutes that he couldn't hold back the tears when I told him to leave. That's how much faith he had in the products, in the atmosphere. Delusion is easy to cultivate. I fear I'll start to receive love poems from that one."

The room was quiet for some moments. Smoke suffocated me.

"So ..." I said, coughing. "Is the Bradfields story real?"

"I don't even know anymore." She kept looking out the window, leaning her lean body against the wall. "Do you have any more questions for me?"

"The Servants outside ..."

"No need to discuss your politics here."

"But isn't your product line a little ... blasphemous for The Org?"

She stubbed the cigar out in her ashtray and sighed. "Like everything, that is for The Org to decide. Anything else?"

"Well, the internship was advertised as paid. I was wondering what the rate was?"

"We pay you in boundless experience."

"Experience?"

"Yes. This will look great on your résumé. I might use you as a degraded fuck toy, too. I'm sure you'll enjoy working here."

"Hang on, Ms Bolt. I need to pay rent. I've already worked two unpaid internships."

"But experience is *priceless*, Bacch. And there is a bakery downstairs. Sometimes they give us freebies. We could pay you in baked leftovers as well."

I stood up & walked out. Another young, bright-eyed graduate sat in reception, waiting her turn. Some men & women stood in the corner, whispering with each other as I left. Most wore suits, but one woman was in a striking red dress, red reading glasses on her nose. Civil Servants.

"Bacch!" screamed Ms. Bolt from behind me. "You lazy freeloader!! *Think of the perks of being my unpaid fuck toy, you NIHILISTIC FILTH!!!*"

I ran out, feeling the pressure of time, of the eviction, of Ms Bolt and the idea of being her unpaid fuck toy. I needed an income to apply for a new place, hopefully with Cristina, as soon as possible.

And what a waste of fuckin time, some of these interviews, some of these companies...

Downstairs, I passed the bakery on the ground floor. I saw all the food on the racks that might be wasted that evening. Bianca once told me that if they wanted to distribute leftovers, even to houseless people, Org health & safety regulations required such onerous packaging that it was never worth the resources, or the risk of breaking the law.

An endless rotation of wasted leftovers.

Ria's family bakery had been going well since The Org announced plans to restrict sugar supplies. People were stocking up freezers full of sugary products. The whole family was pitching in to help run the shop, while Ria was still imprisoned.

I had an idea.

Cristina

There were still road closures along my walk to work from Wynyard Station, from all of the growth and damage. At the plaza entrance to The Org, I couldn't help but stop to look at the pulsing IV trees. Large, rippling trees, though nothing compared to what I'd seen engulf the casino. Vegetative insanity. I bent down to look at the chemical catheter bag, unknown nutrients mixed up in a solution and fed straight into these living things. Up close, the bag reflected my face, my eye, in a bizarre, distorted image. I recoiled at seeing myself so warped, and hurried on inside and up the elevator.

"Ah! Cristina!" said Mr Ogglesworth as I entered our office. He was packing up his desk, folding papers, then unfolding them, then folding them again. "How are you?"

"I'm –"

"I have some unfortunate news, my dear. Our department is to be reshuffled. You'll be moving up to Level 84. Public Relations. I'm sure you'll keep everything running like *cluckwork*, as always."

"But why?"

"The Org has decreed that problem gambling is no longer a problem. Wonderful news, really."

He kept folding and unfolding papers, scrutinising them, then repeating the process.

"Also," he continued, "you're a true believer. It shows. They reward that."

I took what little I had from my desk, said my goodbyes, and took the elevator up to 84. It all looked much the same as Level 19, though there was a little more action going on, people walking back and forth, unhurried. A lady approached me as I walked in. She looked like a mix between Tony Abbot and Margaret Thatcher. I shivered.

"Ah! You must be Cristina, from downstairs? I'm Mrs Ogglesworth."

"Oh! Are you the wife of Mr Ogglesworth from Level 19?"

"No."

"Oh."

"I'm the wife of Mr Ogglesworth from Level 22. Very common name, of course."

"Is it?"

"Essentially, you'll be working on our primary public relations project for now," Mrs Ogglesworth began, leading me through the offices. "Everyone's very excited about it. We want to sell people capital punishment, just like we try to sell them anything. Sex sells. The death penalty is sexy. We must sell it as sexy."

She showed me the tearoom. Mrs Ogglesworth had edited and printed old memes directing workers to clean up, put the dishwasher on at the end of the day, label their food or risk it being thrown out. No plants anywhere.

"It possesses that same climactic, cathartic intensity," she continued, walking back among the cubicles. "A morally complex and divisive distraction. Some sales firms are assisting us, such as Paradisiac. They sell wonderful oysters."

"Excuse me, Mrs Ogglesworth," I said.

"Yes, dear?"

"I ... I don't know if I can work on such a project."

"You have objections, dear?"

"I just don't know what The Org stands for if it is willing to kill."

"The Org kills enemies overseas all the time. We are justified in wiping out villages because religious militants are killed in the process. But we are losing. Look at what happened to our casino, to the safety of Sydney. We must make an example out of such barbarians."

"Well –"

"Do you read the Bible, Cristi?"

Thou shalt not kill.

"Yes, Mrs Ogglesworth. The Bible's message is love."

"We might be reading different bibles. *Eye for an eye.* That's in Leviticus, Exodus, Deuteronomy."

"That's just Old Testament," I said. "In Matthew, this is reneged. Honour and love is the true way. In Peter and Romans, too."

"I'm glad you mentioned Romans, Cristina."

Mrs Ogglesworth closed her eyes in rapture, almost trembling beneath her boxy grey outfit. Her spine stood up a little straighter. She took some deep, audible breaths. Other staff began to take notice.

"Romans 13: *Let everyone be subject to the governing authorities, for there is no authority except that which God has established. The authorities that exist have been established by God. Consequently, whoever rebels against the authority is rebelling against what God has instituted, and those who do so will bring judgement on themselves. For rulers hold no TERROR for those who do RIGHT, but for those who do WRONG. Do you want to be free from fear of the one in authority? Then do what is RIGHT and you will be commended. For the one in authority is God's Servant for your good. But if you do WRONG, be AFRAID, for rulers do not bear the sword for NO REASON. They are God's Servants, agents of wrath to bring punishment on the wrongdoer. Therefore, it is necessary to submit to the authorities, not only because of possible punishment but also as a matter of conscience. This is also why you pay taxes, for the authorities are God's Servants, who give their full time to governing. Give to everyone what you owe them: If you owe taxes, pay taxes; if revenue, then revenue; if respect, then respect; if honour, then honour.*"

Mrs Ogglesworth opened her eyes and let out a small cry from her wide, grinning mouth. She was sweating, clasping her hands as if they were damp towels being wrung out.

"I just *love* that verse. Don't you? Of course you do. If our governing authority decrees a lawful punishment for terrorist wrongdoers, for the Casino Three, then we must obey. If the Org says they die next Friday, then we must obey."

"Next Friday? That seems too soon?"

"The King announced it this morning. Now would you like to get to work, Cristina?"

"Do we know how The Org will be ... administering the execution?"

"The word 'execution' sounds so barbaric, in my opinion. We prefer the proper term here, 'capital punishment', or 'CP'."

"Ok, 'CP'. Do we know how they'll do it?"

"Still classified. Hopefully not by injection. Not barbaric enough, in my opinion. Oh! Here's your desk. We really need to push support for all of this online, with hourly posts across socials, all of them, everywhere. Remember, CP equals sexy. But nothing too sexy. No female nipples in any content."

"Oh. What about ... male nipples?"

"Male nipples, sure. Great. Anyway, the social media manager will be over soon to brief you. Lovely to meet you, Cristina!"

She left me standing at my desk, among countless other desks. In a front corner of the office, a TV provided Media Ochre's news coverage of Party air force exercises and other terrorist threats. I wasn't in the mood to work. I felt sick. I needed air.

The social media manager was approaching me. I excused myself and ran out, down the stairwell to Level 73, through the skybridge park. I didn't know what to do next. I sat beneath a tree. My distorted reflection looked back at me from the little nutrient bag nearby. I recalled the screaming man on the train.

Are you ok?

But there was no one there for me, to tell me everything was ok. No Bacch. No parents. Not even God.

I looked at my phone for some kind of comfort. Instead, it notified me that Neil deGrasse Tyson had been assassinated by terrorists. The world was in mourning. Someone had posted a status with his quote about manufacturing your own meaning of life, creating your own love, your own motivation. Lots of emojis. I put my phone away.

Eventually I found myself back at my desk, listening to the social media strategies and how they should be executed.

Bacch

Bianca the Baker no longer worked at the bakery. I'd been applying for jobs with food service outlets but they all expected me to leave at the first real career opportunity, which would have been valid if I had any real career opportunities.

Thursday. Ten days until eviction. I was hoping she could help me out.

Bianca now worked for the poshest restaurant in Darling Harbour, she told me. Her sales had gone through the roof. It wasn't just the customers buying coke from her. Now it was the cooks. I found her out front on smoko, in a black collared shirt, hair tied back, black dress pants, looking out across the water, to the shops & the other casino & the pedestrian bridge linking everything. You could make out giant vines wrapping themselves around the pylons of the Pyrmont Bridge. Org workers, suspended from the railings, were busy hacking at it all.

It was illegal to smoke here but Bianca went on ahead. Perhaps I'd been too quick to let her go.

"I can always tell," she said, "from how a kid interacts at the door – eye contact, general social presence, body language towards me & others – whether it's gonna be an iPad family or not. Every time."

"Makes sense."

"You watch, when we go in."

"We can just chat out here if you want."

"My break is over." She stubbed out her ciggie.

"I want to help out a friend by working at their bakery," I said, following her in through the terrace seating.

"Isn't that helping yourself?"

A family was checking the menu at the entrance. I was not dressed well enough to be in here.

"Oh hello & *welcome!*" Bianca said to them, grinning like the Cheshire Cat. She bent down to eye level with the son. "And how are you today, young man?"

He barely answered, looking away at something low to the ground nearby.

"Right! Well, just this way, folks."

I had to wait at the bar until she returned from seating them. I ordered a beer.

"So, the bakery caught me selling bags," said Bianca, walking back & pouring drinks. "At least here, the restaurant management knows everyone's on drugs & lets the wheel turn itself. A chef punched a busboy in the face & the busboy was fired for it. Craziness. Y'know?"

She took the drinks over on a circular tray to the family table; a white wine, a bloody mary, and a raspberry lemonade for the youngster. The family had already put the iPad in front of him. His eyes darted around the screen like he was playing the pokies, while the parents gazed out across the harbour.

"See that iPad?" she whispered upon her return.

"Every time, ay?"

"Every time."

"How are things with your man friend?"

"Not bad. Interesting. We're trying an open relationship."

"Oh?"

"Yeah. He's been in Melbourne for a week. A week! I'm in heat, Bacch. I've got the fever. I miss you."

"I miss you too." I drank my beer.

She put her hands on the bar & looked down with a deep sigh.

"Do you have any tips with this bakery situation?" I asked finally.

"Is that really what you came here for?" she asked.

I looked at her.

She looked at me & sighed again. "I may need a favour from you, though."

"Oh?" I finished the beer.

She pounced & grabbed the front of my shirt. I had no choice. She dragged me aside in one motion & flung me through the wide doors of the accessible bathroom. I stumbled; she caught me & we careened into a wall with an eruption of kisses & moans & clawing at each other's clothes. Desperation for satiation. She sat her suddenly bare arse up on the hand railing, hands unbuckling my belt as I ripped at her blouse. I refamiliarised my hands, fingers, lips & tongue with her exposed fields & hidden corners. She spread her legs, already soaked. Bianca always seemed primed, as if life itself constantly seduced her, had her ready & trembling before anyone had even touched her. She guided me in, the frenzy suspended at the tip of ecstatic expectation, before slipping all the way into each other & she screamed so loud I thought they'd break down the door to save us from ourselves.

Where's Cristi, though?

Bianca came quickly & pushed me away. "I need to get back to work," she whispered, though she caught sight of my furious erection. She bent down & shoved a finger up my arse as she swallowed it, freshly coated & glistening wet with her own ejaculate. It almost worked, but I couldn't close my eyes to the reality that we were done & over with each other, and that we were in a toilet stall, though it was one of the nicer ones we'd fucked in. I softened. She stood up & wiped her mouth.

"You're a pussy," she said.

"Cheers."

We adjusted our clothes & walked out at separate intervals, her first. In her absence, I looked at myself in the mirror.

No comment.

When I walked out, Bianca said, "I'm not sure why you asked me for tips about bakeries. I was a shit employee. But good luck."

"Cheers, Bianca. Cheers to you."

I guess I'd just wanted to see her.

Where's Cristi, though?

As I walked out, a girl met my gaze. She sat at one of the tables set for two out in the corner of the terrace, though I hadn't noticed her before. She seemed familiar. Her eyes didn't move from mine as I neared the entrance, near her.

"I know what you did in there," she said from her table.

"Cicely?" It was the blonde bony photographer, from an inspection long ago.

"The whole restaurant heard you. Heard her. All kind of quick, though."

I looked over at the iPad family. They didn't appear to have heard a single thing.

"What are you doing here?" I asked.

"App date."

"Ah."

"But I've been stood up. I've been here for twenty minutes, drinking by myself, no answer from the scumbag. Are you hungry?"

"You want me to replace your date?"

"Look, Bacch. That's your name, right? Bacch, I've been stood up four times in a row on dates arranged online. I message them, and they just ghost me. They leave me on *seen*. Am I that bad?"

"You're gorgeous."

"I know, right? Right! I came here for validation. And then I had to listen to your carry-on in there. Why can't I have that, too? That BEAUTY! *Why can't we all have that?*"

Her voice verged on hysterics, but she caught herself, closed her eyes. Took some deep breaths, inhaling & exhaling slowly. She opened her eyes at me, and smiled.

"Mini-meditation. It's incredible. You should try it."

"Would you like to go on a date with me, right now, Cicely?"

83

But she was looking at someone standing next to me, a slick cunt look about him, with sharp eyes & a well-fitted dress shirt.

"Hi, Cicely?" he said to her. "I'm Patrick, your date. Sorry to have kept you waiting."

"Patrick?" she said.

"Who?" I said.

"I couldn't access Maps or contact you," he continued, ignoring me. "My phone ... Look at this."

This Patrick guy pulled out his mobile. There were several cracks in the screen. Thorned vines of tiny red roses were growing out from the splintered glass. It was incredible.

"You brought me roses?" said Cicely.

"What?"

"They're adorable!"

"Um, yeah," he said, sitting down. "So cute, ay."

"Hey," I said. "I might go."

But they didn't notice me. Kept chatting. Ghosted me. Left me on *seen*. I looked around for Bianca. She was serving someone at the register. I waved. She didn't notice either. I walked off through Darling Harbour, marvelling at the world.

Ria was still locked up.

And I never even got that headshot with Cicely.

Cristina

A field of giant sunflowers had grown up through the tunnels of the city circle train line, reaching for the surface, the sun. Such an inconsiderate act of nature. I was among countless commuters who now took the bus instead, squashed in and standing up. Half the passengers wore facial masks. It took some time to navigate peak hour traffic, with main streets closed for the light rail construction. Thoroughfares like Anzac Parade and George Street still looked like fish with their bellies cut up the middle. I wanted to get off and walk instead, but it took a few more stops before I could wrangle a position closer to the exit doors, through all the bodies.

I wanted to check Mrs Ogglesworth's Bible verses, but my phone was dead. I left my Bible back up the coast – accidentally, of course – but I'd seen one on Bacch's bookshelf. At the apartment, I dropped my bag and went straight to his room. Bacch wasn't home. To get to the shelf I had to kick aside clothes and a mandala drape that had fallen from the wall. The room had a smoky scented texture. A guitar he never played rested in the corner, dust on the fret board.

I found the Bible next to a Quran, several texts on Buddhism of Tibetan, Chinese and Indian streams, Egyptian mythology, history books covering all continents, books of atheistic arguments, and the rest mostly novels and short story collections. Other than the first *Lord of the Rings*, I hadn't read any of these books, hadn't heard of the authors.

I traced a finger down their spines. They seemed like remnants of bygone lives, persisting on shelves like ghosts in words, in spite of technological imposition.

I removed the Bible and opened it.

Dear God.

Pages and pages had been torn out, snipped up, all throughout, seemingly at random. I had never seen a thing like it. I fell onto Bacch's bed. My heart felt twisted. Strangely, I couldn't help but think of faith-ordained mutilation.

I looked up the passage in Romans. It had avoided desecration. Mrs Ogglesworth had quoted it well.

I lay there on his bed for hours, reading, trying to piece together some semblance of truth in the world. The holy words now seemed unfamiliar, their potency withered by literary carnage. I took the Quran down to read as well. I had never actually seen a Quran before. The cover was beautifully ornate, as if plucked from the library of an ancient Arabian king. Someone regal, with real influence ... *unlike our King*. But I couldn't shake the instinct that the book was my enemy, like it could infect me with something, something *other*. I began reading; it, too, had been torn apart. Bacch had been indiscriminate. What was his reason? His fury?

The page numbers ran backwards. I went to the end, which was actually the start. The whole book ran backwards, in line with the Arabic text that accompanied the English translation. Different, yet the tone of the verses I flicked through rang somehow familiar.

I kept reading all kinds of things I'd never considered before. I flicked through the works of Lord Byron, whoever he was. Some books were pure erotica. I opened musky pages dripping with words of indecent passions, many written by women, Anaïs Nin and @talesoflara and others, previously unfamiliar with their names and the nature of their sultry characters' exploits.

They affected me.

I'll never forget my first dream of adolescent iniquity. A handsome lifeguard was drowning in the shallows of the local beach. Not a single person was there to help except me. I looked along the endless shore, sparkling and stretching forever north and forever south. The world was empty but for us. Daytime, yet the stars were out. I pulled him out onto the sand, which was not sandy but smooth, not compact but yielded to our movements. I can still feel how it moved around us, the vivid textures. I was wet, and not from the ocean. At the time I didn't really know what it was, nothing of the biology, barely the vocabulary to explain it. But I knew I liked it.

"I've been waiting for you," said the lifeguard, already missing most of his clothes out of professional and practical necessity. "Come heeeeere ..."

We lay on the beach together for a few languid moments of ecstasy until I woke up, feeling as if I'd taken a warm ocean dip.

"God would be so ashamed of me," I realised.

The sordid memory never faded. I wondered if Bacch ever felt ashamed about his body.

He never came home that night. Eventually I packed up all the books, save for the Anaïs Nin collection, which I took to the couch. I thought of touching myself. Bacch could walk in at any moment, yet somehow that spurred on the idea. It pulled me, inch by inch, seducing myself, desire taking root, blood rushing through me. My fingertips played with page corners. I could feel myself down there, a wet response to nothing but myself, imagination, restless desire.

He could come home any minute.

A knock at the door startled me from my reverie. Gathering myself, I opened up to see Jeffrey, the neighbour from downstairs, hair everywhere, forlorn eyes.

"Oh, hello," he said. "Is Bacch home? I'm just lookin for some lamingtons, but shops are closed. Is Bacch on?"

"No, sorry."

"Ah, k, ah well. Well, pity about the eviction, ay. Where are you going to go?"

"I'm sorry?"

"Didn't you get the letter, darl? Redevelopment. Whole building. Hey, you sure you don't have any lamingtons lying around?"

"Um, no ..."

"No worries, no worries. Thanks luv, seeya soon. Praise The Org."

I closed the door and returned the book to Bacch's shelf. Near my wrist, popping out from beneath some papers, was an envelope torn open. I grabbed it, read it and reread it. EVICTION NOTICE. I microwaved something, ate alone and went to bed. Thoughts of sex, eviction, terrorism, capital punishment, sex, different Bibles, Bacch, dishonesty, my parents, losing your shelter, sex – it all kept me awake long afterwards.

Bacch

A gaggle of piranhas with microphones & cameras blocked most of the entrance to the courthouse, flanked by monolithic sandstone pillars. Reporters with flapping gills looked around for food, for a story, for something. Cameras flashed. Terrorism gets attention.

I was at home, but Kafi was sending me live content. I walked back & forth in the apartment, reading & watching.

Friday. Nine days until eviction.

The key issues of the case were whether or not reading and/or possessing a particular book in public was sufficient to cause fear in people, i.e. to terrorise. Evidence was heard that many Australians were indeed fearful of the books in question & the conflicting beliefs they espouse. Therefore, the defendant had indeed caused fear by bringing them out into the open, at the risk of being read. Plus, the marks on her arms and face were of her own doing, not the Protectors'.

The defence stated that a crime requires both *actus reus,* the actual conduct or action of the crime, and *mens rea*, the criminal intention or knowledge. The defendant, they argued, lacked the latter aspect. The only terror caused was unintentional, and limited to the family who reported Ria for reading multiple religious books at once while in a coffee shop. There was no precedent for prosecuting someone in such a way. Least of all a high school girl. Plus, they argued, the Protectors' fact sheet was not factual, featuring details that never happened, and omitting details that did.

The judge was about to reach a verdict when I heard banging at the door. Aggressive. My heart dropped into my stomach. Some terror seemed to lurk behind the knock, leaking through the gaps around the door, seeping through the wood & the cracks & the warm air getting heavier. Cristi was at work, as far as I knew.

It wasn't a familiar knock, not old mate Jeffrey from downstairs. They banged again. I darted around the apartment, making sure any evidence of contraband was hidden well away.

"Is anyone home?"

It was the voice of a young girl. I gradually approached the door. Knock knock knock again.

I unlocked & opened. She stood there in black polished shoes over white socks that ran up her legs beneath a dark blue plaid skirt. Her top was a white & red uniform with sleeves rolled up a little but not past the elbow. Red, white & blue. A patch over her heart depicted the national crest of The Org, the kangaroo & the emu. She held a large, empty plastic basket.

"Um ... hello?" I peeped.

"Hello!" she blurted. "I'm with The Org Scouts. How are you today?"

"Um ... just fine, thanks."

"Do you have any books you'd like to donate to the burn?"

"The ... burn?"

She smiled even wider. Her hair was tied back in a ponytail. The excessive makeup & beaming red lipstick made each expression even more theatrical.

"We're taking donations of immoral books so we can host community bonfires."

"Community ... *bonfires?*"

"Yes, they're a great way to bring people together during these difficult and ... unprecedented times."

I could hear sounds down the stairwell, a mix of voices and heavy boots.

"What do you mean by immoral?" I asked.

90

"Are you a member? A believer?" Her eyes were wide with hope.

"Um ... yes, yes I am."

"Then you already know. Are you sure you don't have anything you'd like to donate to the cause? Even just a history textbook that's taking up some space?"

"Um, look," I began, but I was lost for words. The Scout peered past me into the apartment. I moved to take up more space in the frame.

"At the very least," she said, in a strange new tone, "I'd really consider donating that painting there."

I turned to look – the koala, sitting on the cross, amongst the fire.

"No," I said. "A friend gave that to me."

"It doesn't look so friendly."

She was still smiling. I remained silent.

"Do you have a Bible?"

"Yes, yes of course." I said it casually, but I was sweating.

"May I see it?"

"Ah ... One second, please."

I felt gravity flip a few times. I walked back to my bedroom, checked the floorboard was in place over the secret stash spot, grabbed the Bible from the bookshelf, and opened it. Snipped up. I pulled out a few that were hanging too loose off the spine, and closed it with a thud.

I held it up as I returned to the doorframe.

"Ah, excellent," she said. "Though that edition looks out of date. May I have a look?"

I stopped a few paces away from her & the doorway. "No."

"No?"

"It was my father's. Why do you care, sorry?"

"The Org can provide you with a new version of the Holy Book. It's quite up to date."

The book was heavy in my hand. "I thought the word of God never changed, that He created timeless perfection."

"Timeless perfection ..." she mused. "And yet, we are all mortal sinners."

We stood there, facing each other. Voices & boots still drifted up. Her lipstick glistened.

"Right," she said at last. "Well, if you're sure there's nothing?"

"Nothing," I said, though my voice seemed far away.

"Ok. We'll leave you to it, mister."

She turned to leave but dawdled for a brief moment. She looked back, into my eyes. Her gaze sparkled with awe & conviction.

"God bless The Org. God bless Australia. God bless Freedom."

She turned on her heels & disappeared, skipping down the stairs. The voices & boots lingered, became echoes, soon receding. I stared into the stairwell for who knows how long. Eventually I locked the door & walked out to the balcony. My hands gripped the lattice railing. White knuckles. I looked down at Elizabeth Street. It was teeming with Protectors escorting Org Scouts & handling book donations, throwing them into large trays on the backs of small trucks parked in loading zones. There were no bonfires, not yet.

Would they come back here?

I went back to the couch & grabbed my phone to find info on whatever was happening, but when the lock screen vanished, the verdict for Ria was just one voice memo away.

Cristina

I had nothing to wear.

"No," had been my initial response to Patrick. I didn't want my first date in Sydney to be with him, the human manifestation of a pelican. I mean, he was almost good-looking, if you'd never heard him open his mouth.

We were in the elevator, all squeezed together, he against me. Wendy wasn't there, just other men in suits. His hand brushed mine. It was probably an accident, but I moved my hand away anyway. My hand accidentally brushed the older gentleman's on my other side. He looked down at me, winked and smiled. I looked straight ahead.

"Sorry, Patrick."

"But you said you're not doing anything tonight," continued Patrick. "It's Friday. You need someone to show you around, show ya how we do it here in the city."

"No, it's ok, thanks."

"I'll pay for your dinner. I'm not an animal."

"Well ..."

"Well ...?"

"Well, that's not it. I can pay, it's fine."

"Great," he said. "I've already made the reservation."

"I haven't said yes."

"You just did. Don't be such a tease, Cristina."

The elevator opened up on my floor. I stepped out.

"I'll see you at The Snakepit tonight," said Patrick. "Should be enough time before lockout. Dad said there's a development proposal for the whole block. Might not be around for long. Oh, and Cristina? Dress up a little bit."

The elevator doors closed, almost squashing his pelican beak.

I really was going to stay in. I really was. I had no idea where Bacch was or when he'd be home. He had half a bottle of red wine open on the counter, probably from watching Ria's trial. I poured a glass and sat out on the balcony, toes in the coarse astroturf, watching people live in the big city. It would normally be impossible to see the Harbour Bridge from here, but it's as if some days the buildings sway, like coral in the waves, allowing glimpses of different sights at different times. The city is a lucky dip. So much happening that anything could happen. Here I was. Alone. Imagining it all. The wine went down. Patrick was good-looking, for a human pelican. Life can be a bit of a struggle. I had never been on a proper date, at least not with someone I didn't really know. The thought of it made me thirstier. I poured another glass.

Patrick sent me an address. 'The Snakepit' didn't show up on Maps.

Was such entitled talk like his normal? As if he couldn't understand the word NO? Was it so difficult to respect someone?

I should go give him a piece of my mind. Just because I exist doesn't mean I'm a tease, doesn't mean I owe anyone anything. I didn't ask for God to create me. And what would I wear?

I took the wine to my room. The blood of Christ.

I got naked in front of the mirror. The body of Christ.

My body.

Dress up a little bit.

If I go out, how I look is for myself.

It was so hot that my feet were swollen. I took a cold shower to calm my body down, before dressing it up. Chucked a few poses in front of the mirror. Finished the wine.

Let's go.

Bacch

Kafi's voice memo began with some muffled sounds, until things got clearer, but still kinda tinny and distant. The judge was delivering the verdict, directly addressing Ria.

"You're a danger to my children, reading things like that in public. It's a gateway to other ideologies, other ways of thinking. Next thing, you'll be in some professor's study smoking reefer, and who knows what else. Now, it says here you've got anxiety and depression. Boo hoo. You wrote in your submission that you were mistreated by Protectors? Boo hoo. 'I was violently arrested, causing injuries that no one has yet treated.' Boo hoo. 'Protectors stripped me naked except for my shoes, on a Surry Hills street between the open doors of their van as people walked by. They made me spin and squat.' BOO HOO. If you don't have any prohibited items on you, next time you just hold out your arms, let them search you, and you get to walk away. If you have nothing to hide, you have nothing to fear. That is how we operate. Everyone is a potential criminal. Look at you. You were nominated for the Servant of Education's Award last year. The *Servant's Award* ... tsk tsk. Look at you now. What a fall from grace."

I couldn't believe what I was hearing, and he was still going. This was a real judge.

"You won't be leaving here to brag to your friends. No one is above the rules of The Org. Not even the King. I'm going to convict you for a short holding stint. You need to learn your lesson. Shouldn't be a problem for such an 'intellectual'. *Pfft*. Not so smart now. And if I ever see you in my courtroom again, I will smash you. I will obliterate you."

And that was it. Guilty. Ria was in a cell. All the papers owned by Media Ochre were covering it, saying the verdict was a victory for freedom & peace. It was sickly strange. I didn't know what to do about anything. I wasn't even surprised at the verdict. The law was not the same as morality. They were launching an appeal, at least.

Kafi sent another voice memo, just a short one.

"Fuckin dawgs. The judge tried to humiliate her, but he only humiliated himself."

Ria's family bakery wouldn't accept me. I said it could be just another unpaid internship, but still, no. They didn't need a saviour. They just needed their daughter back.

Bianca's old bakery didn't give me a job, either. Instead, I went round back in the arvo, paid off her replacement, Oscar, with a beautifully rolled joint as he was cleaning & closing up. I took home bags of leftovers like Santa Claus slinking through the shadows on Christmas Eve. Corruption at all levels of society. Unavoidable.

I had been searching for news on the book 'donations' & The Org Scouts since that unwelcome visit. Other than a few mentions on socials, the internet was blank for it. I'd tried calling Hari to ask if he could find anything using his VPN connection, but it kept going to voicemail, no call backs.

No burn, no fires.

What's coming?

I took the bags back to the apartment, laid the donuts & slices & buns & bread loaves & scrolls & rolls & pastries & pies all out on serving plates far less fancy than Ms Bolt's oyster tray, but they still did the trick. The sweet goods had a strangely inflated demand, but also high prices due to inflation & sugar taxes. Not everyone could afford them. I bought the end-of-day goods at almost zero dollars & could sell them in the streets. Paying no tax on revenue, I could set the prices wherever. The country needs tax revenue, I know. *But where does it go?*

I hoped Cristi would approve.

She still wasn't home. Something was wrong. Or maybe she was just out enjoying herself.

Staff drinks?

I balanced the final donut atop my sugary pyramid. The black market of resold sugar awaited.

If you worried about everything that could happen whenever you made a decision, instead of getting excited by what could happen, you'd stay in your house wrapped in bubble wrap, hooked up to a feeding tube & an orgasm machine, inside a blast-proof safe, in front of a screen.

That Friday night I sold most of it just within the building. Tenants were lined up & down the stairs, less than eight days before we were all to be evicted. Jeffrey was first in line. Still *stingin*. He bought half the gear. The scarcity of affordable baked goods & the general fear of being killed outside in a terrorist attack meant demand was high in here.

"Hey, Jeffrey," I asked before he went back to his front door.

"Yeeah brudda?"

"Did an Org Scout come to your apartment this week?"

"Yeah, yeah, she did ay."

"What did she want?"

"Books. Ha! Imagine me, having fuckin *books*. Gave me a new Bible though, how good ay."

"How good ay."

"Found a new place to live yet, Bacch?"

"No, I haven't."

"Might have to join the services of The Org, the way things are going."

"How are things going, Jeffrey?"

"Yeah, look, not good, not good." Jeffrey was staring at the floor, but looked up suddenly with a smile. "Better now with these lamingtons ayyy."

"Ayyy."

"I mean, why won't The Org just let us run a regulated market for this stuff?" said Jeffrey. "We'd be safer knowing exactly what we're getting. Not that I don't trust you, y'know ..."

"All good," I said. "I get you. Why shouldn't they let the people indulge in sugary sweets, get together for tea & bickies with friends, even if it's not so healthy?"

"Ayyy."

I brought a tray down to the ground floor for Mrs Clancy. She walked out, actually wrapped in bubble wrap, hooked up to an IV feeding tube. I didn't wait to look around for the orgasm machine. She stocked up, underpaid me as if she hadn't, and closed the door. Such is life.

By midnight I'd sold the last of the finger buns to people loitering around Strawberry Hills. Not much else was happening on a Friday night, with lockouts and curfews. But there were four other bakeries in the area that I could visit on the way home. Bakers generally started their shifts at night so everything would be fresh for the morning. I visited them all. One place turned me away, one was still completely closed and dark with silhouettes of trees growing inside, and the other two sold me more bags than I could carry. Somehow I managed to get it all back into the apartment by 1am after a few trips up and down the stairs.

Cristi still wasn't home when I got back. I messaged her but fell asleep before any reply.

Cristina

The address led me down a dark alleyway in Darlinghurst. No distinguishing features other than the cracks in the ground where vines with beautiful bright flowers climbed up the grimy brick walls. As I ventured deeper, I wondered if this was safe, or if Patrick had led me astray.

A neon chandelier came to life from the darkness up ahead, hanging from a wrought-iron fixture several storeys above. Its glow spilled across a big fella in a ruffled suit, loose tie, buttons barely buttoned, and a bowler hat. Smoke curled around him, face unseen beneath the hat. Noir nonchalance.

I stopped. Seeing it closer, seeing it move, I realised a gorgeous, giant black snake was wrapped around the man's shoulders, along an arm, writhing, looking around here and there.

"Cristina!"

I spun around to see Patrick walking down the alley.

"Hi, Patrick. Hey, have you been here before?"

"Oh my god, you look so sexy tonight!"

"Thanks. You look ... Have you ever been here?"

"No, no, I just heard my dad talking about it on the phone, about the proposal. An apartment block and a grocery – woah, what is *that*?"

He looked past me at the bouncer and his snake.

"You don't like snakes?" I asked. "They're beautiful creatures."

"Perhaps we should go somewhere else," said Patrick.

I could feel the wine. Ignoring Patrick, I walked toward the doors. He caught up. The snake glowed in the neon. I remembered, when I was really little, thinking that snakes were scaly, as if they had a hard surface. But Dad caught one near the house one day, a harmless one, but big. He let me touch it. It was soft and smooth, muscles moving beneath the skin.

Patrick took out his ID. The bouncer chuckled, opened the door and just let us in.

As we walked down a curling staircase, Patrick whispered, "That was illegal. Every licensed venue in Sydney has to diligently review, accept and record a valid piece of ID. How do they get away with that?"

The staircase opened out to a vast underground room with a circular bar as the centrepiece, giant branches and rainforest growth everywhere, the furniture and layout all nestled along with it. The place was crowded with patrons in bizarre fashions, loud with chatter and jazztronica. Something about the lighting made the walls and branches shimmer and move. I didn't think open flames in venues were legal either, but there were candles lit everywhere, soft against lounges and leaves. But then other corners sprouted ferns and fronds that glowed with a.m. neon. Dark and disorienting.

We approached a spare table near the bar, low to the ground, the legs covered in vines.

"I never thought a place like this would exist here," I said.

"I think we should go."

"We just got here. Didn't you say your dad recommended it?"

"I overheard him on the phone about it. I didn't realise ... I don't know if it's even legal for us to be here."

"Hi, y'all." A beautiful waiter, a tall boy with eyeliner, high cheekbones, bright hair, pulled our seats out for us. I sat. Patrick hesitated.

"You're our waiter?" he said.

"Yes, darl. Any problem?"

Patrick sat.

"What can I get for you?" asked the waiter.

"Menu?" said Patrick.

"They're there in front of you."

Indeed they were. I let slip a smile.

"Oh, of course," said Patrick. "Cristina, what would you like to drink?"

"Sir," I said to the waiter. "Can I please have ... absinthe?"

"No no no," said Patrick. "How about a ... cosmopolitan?"

"I'll have absinthe," I repeated. "He can have the cosmopolitan. Thank you."

"I can choose my own drink."

"So can I. Absinthe, please."

"Sugar and all?" asked the waiter, with a toothy grin of glee.

"Sugar and all."

"Coming right up."

He went back to the bar, where a woman was sitting, alone, though they chatted as if they knew each other, looking over at us.

"You know sugar isn't good for you?" said Patrick, half his face lit by neon, the other half by candlelight. "The Org is going to restrict –"

"You know alcohol isn't good for you?" I said, looking around the place.

"He didn't even take my order ..."

Oh.

It wasn't the lighting that was making everything appear like it was moving. There were snakes everywhere along the branches, the vines, letting us glimpse them here and there. Wild place.

Patrick was saying something.

"Sorry, what?" I said.

"Are you distracted?"

"Yes. There are snakes all around you."

"Oh my, you're right!" His eyes betrayed horror.

"What's wrong with snakes?" I said. "Always the villains. The devil in the Garden of Eden. A symbol of chaos from the underworld, but also of life, of ... fertility. Disney just needs to cast a snake as the good guy."

Patrick still seemed horrified. He didn't know what to say. Perhaps I was suited to PR at The Org.

Oh my God. A Disney film about The Org. Eww.

I could still feel the wine working. Absinthe would be interesting. Patrick was saying things again.

People kept walking back and forth, tripping and dancing and taking each other by the hand. I glanced at the waiter and his lady friend, looking over at me and smiling. On the bar, a fountain dripped water from a tap over the sugar cube spoon, dissolving it all into the absinthe solution. He operated it all like an old sci-fi teleportation machine.

"... And that's when we realised, I was high on life, all the time," continued Patrick. "So, my family doctor prescribed some stuff to help balance me out."

"That doesn't sound healthy," I said.

"It's legal. It has to be healthy."

I saw the waiter spinning between the rushing bodies in coats and corsets and miniskirts and multicoloured irises and insane feathery fashions of the past and future. He popped out of the human current and handed us –

"Absinthe for the lady, and a cosmopolitan for the ... boy."

"Thank you," I smiled.

"I didn't order a cosmopolitan," protested Patrick.

"You asked for a cosmo. She asked for absinthe. So! Food?"

Patrick continued to argue. A human pelican. Snakes in my gut.

Why am I here? Am I so desperate?

I drank the absinthe, all in one gulp. It was smooth but burned. They both looked at me. I looked at them.

I vomited on the table.

"Oh ... my ... god, honey," said the waiter, passing me fistfuls of serviettes and wiping the table down with his tea towel. Patrick fell back off his chair, some vomit on his nice shirt. Snakes hissed. People laughed.

The pelican stood.

"Come on, Cristina," he said. "Let's get you out of here."

I wiped my mouth and chin. "Me? I'm staying. This place is amazing."

"Cristina, we can't stay now. Responsible Service of Alcohol laws prohibit –"

"Darl, if anyone's intox here, you're the one who fell off your chair. This chica is just a bit ill, yeah?"

"Can I please order some dinner?" I said. "I'd like to actually enjoy myself tonight."

Patrick stared at me. "You're a disgrace to The Org."

He walked off up the stairs, out of the jungle and into the jungle.

"I'm so sorry," I said to the waiter. "I don't think he's my type."

I tried to crack a smile, but my body was still rattled from the upheaval. Alcohol is actual poison, yet we drink it.

The waiter grinned. "That was amazing! Except him. He was shitty. My name is Mikael. Let's get you off this table. Wanna come sit at the bar with us, or just quarantined in a corner by yourself?"

"Bar, if that's ok."

I sat next to the woman I'd seen Mikael speaking with. Tight black dress with a deep plunge gap, tiny silver lightning bolt on a necklace nestled between her breasts. Eyes running me up and down.

"That was quite a show," she said with a sharp smile. She seemed in her early forties. "Will you be performing another?"

"Hope not. I'm so embarrassed."

"I'm Zira."

"Cristina."

Zira nodded. "Can I get Mikael to get you a water or something?"

"Do you have apple juice?"

Mikael laughed and dodged another bartender, moving toward some branches growing around a pole at the bar. He reached with the smooth control of a dancer, hand grasping for a bright red apple, plucked only after the stem of the fruit yielded to the pull. Mikael proceeded to put it through a juicer but the buzz of it was barely heard above the chatter and music.

"What brings you here, Cristina?" asked Zira.

"I was on a date."

"Did you like that man?"

"No, to be honest."

"Then why go out with him?"

"I don't know ... I just wanted to go out. Do something different. Something new."

"Have you ever puked on a date?"

"I never had too many dates."

"Boyfriends?"

"One. Back home. He wasn't ... It didn't work out."

Zira bit her lower lip. "What do you mean?"

"It was too much about virginity – him trying to lose his, me trying to keep mine. We did it, kinda. A few times. Too wrapped up in what we'd learned from The Org, from everyone. We could have made it magical; we just never knew how."

Mikael presented the fresh apple juice in a tall glass, slight froth on top. He reminded me of Bacch – but more flamboyant, less brooding. An undeniably feminine flair. I think androgynous is the word. I liked it.

"You know," he said, "my sex therapist friend told me you can't even get a booking for like six months plus. What does that tell you?"

He had a glass of something on ice. We three cheers'd and drank. Definitely not following Responsible Service of Alcohol laws.

AW. Best apple juice ever.

Mikael asked for food orders, and if I was feeling better. I felt amazing. After much deliberation, Zira and I decided to share nachos and a bottle of Bradfield Manor Vintage, whatever that meant – good wine, hopefully. And it was. I was starting to get the hang of this. Cheers again.

"How did you find The Snakepit?" asked Zira.

"Patrick had heard about this place from his dad," I said. "Something about a development proposal."

"What?" Zira turned on me.

"I don't know." The words came out in a rush. "Said it might not be around much longer. That's all he said." I looked away and drank.

Eventually Zira sighed and said, "I'm part-owner here. I have another business, where Mikael works for me, but he fills in here when needed."

"What business is that, Zira?"

"The business of desire, young Cristina. An agency of aphrodisiacs. Naughtiness, disguised."

Mikael was at his cocktail station, cutting a passionfruit in half. He sliced so that the seeds and juices stayed contained in their respective halves, not just spilling out uncontrollably across the wet cutting board.

"Oh. Well, I'm ... in the Program, at The Org. Ugh, that sounds so lame, in a place like this ..."

Zira drank her wine, looking out at the lightshow running across the heaving crowd. "We're now working with The Org, too, in fact. Like everyone. Which is why I would know about a development proposal, if there was one. We just do what we have to do, Cristina. There are Servants here, now, all the time."

"Oh? Do you think they'll recognise me? Should I not –"

"Don't worry yourself. Look, he's a Servant." She pointed over to a man in a suit, unbuttoned shirt, dancing with everyone.

"He's here all the time," continued Zira. "And over there – oh ..."

Her eyes went dark before continuing.

"She's the Servant for Bureaucracy. I haven't seen her here before ... She's close with the King."

Zira pointed out a tall woman in a brilliant red gown and slanted red sunglasses. Sitting by herself near a corner, watching, sipping a drink.

"Hm," said Zira, looking around. "There are actually quite a few here tonight. More than usual."

Zira's breathing was shallow, but she seemed to catch herself, flashed me half a smile, and drank more. I tried to read her without being too obvious. Her eyes became vague, as if distracted. I couldn't help but notice the way her dress moved and slipped and wriggled as she crossed her legs, and then changed them back, every now and again. Her lips looked like they could cause trouble. I had some more wine. And nachos. Such good nachos. Messy.

When I headed to the bathroom, I had to push aside giant ferns and dodge peacock feathers growing out the arse of a man in an extravagant three-piece paisley suit. I stepped aside for a flowing red gown – it was the Servant for Bureaucracy. She walked to the bathroom ahead of me and held the door open.

"Thanks," I said, but I don't think she heard me. The bathroom was packed. Two women and two guys all tumbled out of one cubicle, laughing. I wedged through to a free stall and closed it, though the lock didn't work. Above the toilet ran a glass shelf, I guess to put your things on. Sitting, I listened to overlapping voices, loud snorting on my left, gasping and moaning on my right. I finished in a hurry.

At the sink, my reflection looked back. I didn't recognise her so easily, as if this version of me had lived a different life to mine, and here we found ourselves, catching a glimpse of each other. I put my hand up to hers, the mirror between us. Could we swap? What was her life like? What was my life like?

Someone bumped me, walking past, and I lost balance for a moment.

The Servant appeared next to me again – sunnies in her hand, checking herself out. She saw me looking, sunnies back on, walked out. The two girls gasping reached fever pitch. I lingered, pretending to fix my hair, listening to them yelp. When they subsided, I walked out.

Time felt odd in there that night, like I wasn't aware of it, or it wasn't aware of me. Those are the nights you remember, or at least you wish you could. Zira and Mikael and I drank wine and talked of the dreams

106

we had for ourselves, our passions, our fantasies, all of which I realised I had very few of. They had plenty. We laughed and let ourselves lean on each other with the light brush of a forearm or a few fingertips.

"And what is your passion, Miss Cristina?" asked Zira.

I took a long sip. "I'm not so sure. I'm becoming less and less sure of many things."

"What were you so sure of before," asked Mikael from behind the bar, "that you're not so sure of now?"

"I'm not even sure of that," I laughed. "Moving here, working for The Org, finding places like this, meeting my ... housemate, it's like I'm waking up from a dream that I still remember vividly, caught between waking and sleeping. Like everything you get told as a kid is a lie. Do you ever feel like that?"

"Honey, 100%," said Mikael. "The banks, the church, aged care, even the cricket league. They're all under Royal Org Commission, everything our parents ever believed in and trusted in our trustworthy society, all corrupt, and we're too impotent or laid back or immune to the constant fucking slaps to the face, desensitised to the constant spit from the smiles up above, to bother doing anything about it." He skewered an olive with a toothpick and chomped it.

Zira sighed, looking into her drink. "Too small in the shadows of the titans and the tyrants." She straightened up. "But you must have some interests, Cristina."

"Men or women?" cackled Mikael. "Fuck I'm *sorry darl,* I'm in a mood, you know."

"That's alright, Mikael. I'm interested in ..." I crossed my legs, right over left. Zira watched me. I wondered if I looked like her when she did it. "It's just that ... I was always told it was wrong, but everything wrong seems right, and everything right seems wrong."

"Well *I'm* interested in *you,*" said Mikael, eyes locked, smiling so openly.

I remembered the saloon thoughts, Bacch and this woman, going at it behind the bar. I smiled at Mikael.

"But your *passion*," said Zira. "There must be something in you, begging to happen."

I looked out across the madhouse venue, the underground forest, snakes still everywhere. I crossed my legs back, left over right.

"I don't know my passion yet, but I know I'm passionate."

"Ooft, cheers to that, y'all!" said Mikael, raising his glass. We all connected, arms up for a moment as we shared those big eyes and lil smiles. We finished our drinks.

"If you'd like," said Zira, "Mikael is taking me to a little party tonight. Intimate. You can come, if you want."

"Oh?"

"Have you been to any feisty fiestas in the big city, Cristina?"

"Not exactly."

"Watch out," said Mikael, forever grinning. "Zira took me to my first swingers party."

"Oh," I said, crossing my legs back again, right over left. "Um, what kind of party will tonight be?"

Someone bumped me rushing past. I looked past them. People were streaming toward the exit. Each of us looked around. Cocktails had been left unfinished on tables. Some people still sat laughing or danced on, but more and more patrons looked around and gathered themselves, eyes bewildered and nervous.

Looking back toward the door, several figures walked down into the venue, parting the sea of fanciful bodies rushing in the opposite direction.

"Fuck," whispered Zira.

Protectors, all clad in riot gear, dark visors over their eyes, descended the stairs between leaves and fronds and escapees. The Protectors did not rush. They were calm. There were at least thirty of them, led by a huge Protector with a sawed-off shotgun. He moved steadily, looking at every detail of the venue.

The music cut to silence. The DJ grabbed his headphones and fled to the bottlenecked exodus. The chatter throughout the venue subsided. Even the glassies, bartenders, everyone moved to escape. The unbuttoned Servant from earlier, brow furrowed, cheeks flushed, was moving toward the door. A Protector grabbed him.

"Hey! What are you doing? Unhand me!"

Protectors grabbed a few other people trying to exit, men and women in suits and dresses and colours and jewelled chains. All protested in the name of The Org.

The Servant for Bureaucracy was back in her seat on the other side of the large, low-ceilinged room, in red, smiling.

"Where is the licensee?" called the massive Protector, now metres away from the bar.

A man and a woman, both in collared white shirts and earpieces in, walked over. They glanced at Zira. She stayed seated at the bar, watching. Eyes aflame. Lips clenched.

"I'm licensee," said the woman, removing her earpiece. "He's the venue manager."

The Protector looked them up and down, hand on the hilt of his shotgun. "A young man leaving your establishment earlier, a worker in the Program, informed us of a severe breach of Responsible Service of Alcohol laws here."

Zira, Mikael and I all looked at each other.

That pelican.

"We haven't been shaken down in years," said the venue manager.

"We're just here to ensure you're sticking to your licensing requirements," said the Protector. "We just want everyone to be *safe.*"

The Servant from the dancefloor tried to wriggle free. The Protector holding him twisted his arm. The Servant screamed. "Please! Please ..."

"You haven't even installed any pokies," continued the shotgun Protector. "Just all of this ... illegal nature."

He ripped a leaf from a vine with his black gloved hands, studied it, then tore it up. The pieces drifted to the ground.

I looked over to the Servant in red. She was refreshing her lipstick, pouting and rubbing her lips together.

"Show us your office," continued the Protector. "We need all of the security footage, now."

Another Protector, with his semiautomatic rifle and shield, stepped forward. The venue manager marched with him to a door hidden in the wall. He unlocked it. They entered and disappeared from view. The door closed.

Everyone just stood there. The Protectors didn't move. The captured Servants squirmed against the uniforms that held them. Zira and Mikael waited, bodies rigid.

The Protector emerged from the office door with a hard drive. He nodded to the other Protectors. The venue manager followed, his eyes bloodshot, cheeks puffy, head down, limping.

"I don't think it's fair to blame anyone but yourselves," announced the Protector to the whole room. "There are rules in place. We want people to have fun. But you must obey the law. You must obey The Org. If you can't spend money making your venue safer, if you can't stop patrons harming their bodies with shots and doubles, and bartenders drinking your own stock, well, that's a decision for you, but it's not fair to blame The Org."

"Get fucked," said Zira, standing up. "Get absolutely fucked."

All heads snapped toward her. She maintained her stance.

"Ms Bolt," a voice called. All heads snapped toward the Servant for Bureaucracy. She stood and approached the group. "Certain Servants enjoy your hospitality, your wines, your oysters, your snakes with no permits. Certain Servants ..." She looked at the unbuttoned, sweating

110

official, held tightly from behind. "Certain Servants don't seem capable of *serving*. But not everyone is so two-faced."

She continued walking, looking now at me. "There are those who truly believe in The Org, in living a pure, civilised, regulated, unadulterated life of economic efficiency. This hole of moral destitution is no longer compatible with Australia under Org rule. We are progressing for the better, Ms Bolt."

"What's this development prop–" began Zira, but the Servant stepped forward and held her index finger up in front of Zira's face.

"Ssshhhh ..."

They stared each other down. Then the Servant smiled, and looked at me. She put her red glasses back on.

"Well," she said. "It's past my bedtime."

The Servant for Bureaucracy turned to leave, her gown flying out behind her. She paused next to the shotgun Protector.

"Do it," she said to him. "And her young girlfriend there."

As the red gown disappeared upstairs, past the captured Servants, she called out, "See you all at The Org on Monday!"

The shotgun Protector took a moment. His mouth turned into a smile. "Barkeep! Bottles of your most expensive."

Mikael looked at Zira. "But RSA laws state we can't serve bottles –"

"Just give me the fucking bottles," he repeated.

Mikael's breathing quickened, glancing between Zira, the Protectors and the top shelf.

"He's not breaching RSA for *you*," said Zira.

"And yet how many drinks has he had this evening?" said the Protector. "Well, we have all the security footage."

The venue manager still hung his beat-up head. I think he was crying. Mikael didn't move.

The Protector sighed. "Well. Line them up!"

The other Protectors sprang into movement, dragging their writhing captives so their backs were against the bar, bending them backwards so that their heads were facing up, squeezed securely between gloves, twisting and shaking. They grabbed Zira and forced her into the same position.

The Protector put his huge hand on the bar and jumped over. He grabbed bottles from the top shelf, barely inspecting the labels, handing them along to the other Protectors, who unscrewed them and began to pour burning waterfalls into choking, spluttering, screaming faces and mouths.

"No!" I leaped toward Zira but two Protectors grabbed me from behind. Their uniforms chafed against my skin. I felt like vomiting again.

"Is this what you want?" the Protector spat from behind the bar. "*Is this what you want?* You think we *like doing this?* Hippies, fucking *heathens ...*"

Mikael cowered against the wall. He flinched as the Protector jumped back over, and squared up against me.

"I work at The Org too!" I said, high pitched as tears welled inside me. "Please!"

"Well, missy," said the mouth of the Protector, his eyes still hidden behind the visor. "You really should know better, shouldn't you?"

"But ..."

"Shhh, it's ok. You'll learn, now. Good girl."

The Protectors began to force me toward the bar. My body tried to escape. I kicked my leg out and hit the big guy right in the groin. My foot hit something like a protective cup, but it mustn't have been on properly because he stumbled back, doubled over. The two behind me froze, clutching me hard. All the others stopped pouring and looked up at us.

I still couldn't move. They had me.

"*Fuck you all!*" spluttered Zira. Her Protectors returned their focus and kept pouring. Her body writhed again. Waterboarded with tequila.

The Protector stood, holding his shotgun, pointed at me. His visor reflected my matted hair, my miserable face, the bewildered eyes. His gun stared at me. There was no reflection there, just emptiness. My little body went limp at the sight of it.

Zira's captors stopped again to look up.

My own captors still held me.

The Protector held the sawed-off shotgun straight out at my face.

Movement above.

From a branch that bloomed full and thick with life, a gigantic head descended, followed by a muscular serpentine body that filled the air between the Protector and me. Light danced from its scales in rainbow flashes. Ancient reptilian eyes confronted the sawed-off. The serpent stared down the barrels, then moved its head higher to confront the Protector.

He just stood there.

The serpent watched and never looked away. The Protector slowly put a hand to his visor. It retracted up into his helmet, revealing his face, shotgun still cocked and outstretched. He looked like any man, any father, any son – my brother – anyone in a uniform.

Still, the serpent stared, calm. Still.

Bacch

I woke up to piss & Cristina still wasn't home. I couldn't get back to sleep for a long while. Eventually dozed off & had a REM sleep dream where I was walking over a cobblestone bridge, crossing a moat to a giant castle wall, the King's castle, but it was a fun park, a carnival, a circus. Border Protectors checked my passport at the ticket gate. The Aussie flag flapped atop the turrets. No other flags.

Sniffer dogs & Protectors were waiting inside, but they were strangely swapped. The dogs were standing upright, animal confidence in uniform, holding leashes with human Protectors at the end, on all fours, sniffing, naked but for their collars. They busted Hari – I hadn't even realised he was there, but hey, it's a dream. They dragged him away. I avoided the crawling authorities & waded deeper into the fun park, but it was just poker machines, slots on slots on slots, electric colours scrolling like social media feeds, bright screens burning, hope but no promise.

All the rides were closed. All the rollercoasters & carousels, huge & rusted. Fish lay dead in all the garden ponds, all the water rides. We weren't allowed to do anything & there wasn't much to do. There was a replica Sydney Opera House. Horse races were being projected up onto the sails. I couldn't find the exit, just more pokies, so fuck it, I sat down at More Chilli & put $50 through & lost it & put in another fiddy & I felt Cristina touch my shoulder, but when I turned around, I lost her, too.

I woke up & had to piss again & she still wasn't home.

Cristina

Still, the serpent stared, calm. Still.

The Protector returned the sawed-off shotgun to his side. "Let's go."

No one made the first move. The serpent remained, watching.

"Let's go," he repeated.

The Protectors dropped the bottles, gathered their riot gear and the footage, and moved toward the stairs to the exit, past more and more snakes in branches and vines. The serpent lingered. Everyone else straightened up off the bar, coughing through each breath, eyes bloodshot, hair sticking to their faces, wet with liquor. Liquid bubbled and spilled from the open necks of the dropped bottles across the venue floor. The Servants left silently, wiping their faces, pausing at the top of the stairs to see if Protectors were still around outside. None. They left.

The serpent was gone.

The venue manager ran to the office then stormed out with his bag, in tears.

Mikael was still crouched down behind the bar, legs pulled up under his chin. Zira came to me and hugged me.

"I'm so sorry," she said. She coughed. I felt it against my chest. We held each other. Her black dress was damp and sticky and reeked.

"What do you think happened," I asked, "with that Protector?"

"Fuck knows. Maybe he had some humanity left. Childhood snake memory. Fuck him."

The licensee grabbed a dark bottle and walked to the office. I couldn't imagine wanting to drink liquor after having it relentlessly poured in your face.

"Mikael, get up," said Zira when we parted. "That was ... Mikael! Get up. Fuck this. We're leaving too. I'll sort something to get everything cleaned and fixed. We're ok. We're ok. I'll get your things, Mikael. Don't leave, Cristi." Our gazes linked up. Her eyes betrayed a harrowed wilderness. "Cristi, please don't leave."

She went into the office. Mikael didn't look at me. He removed his tea towel from his waist, ran a hand through his hair, and tried to tidy up the bar, wiping up where people's heads had been. I picked up the bottles and put them on the bar. I went around to tables to collect all the drinks left by fleeing patrons.

"You don't have to clean," called Zira when she re-entered. "I just ordered a crew in to fix it up."

"It's ok," I said, stacking up rescued glasses, hands shaking.

She took out a white vial, looking around the venue, coughing. "No, it's not ok. None of this is ok. They treat us like children. They waste our money. They take our environment. I'll never be one of them. I'll never be one of them. Just let us drink and dance and fuck who we want. Just leave us with our dancefloors. Take everything else, but just leave us the music. Where did that DJ go? Where's the fucking DJ?"

"Honey, Zira," said Mikael. He walked out from behind the bar, toward her. "It's ok."

"You didn't just drown!" Zira had a small spoon. She opened the vial, scooped and snorted, her head held back. Her long, wet hair flopped as she shook her head. "I'm sorry, Mikael."

"Me too."

"Stop cleaning," she said. "Let's go."

We walked up the stairs, back into the Darlinghurst alleyway. It felt like the world had been turned upside down again, like a snow globe in the dark. I had not adjusted to the new gravity.

We were on our way to Zira's apartment. Swept up in the evening. I walked with them through Darlinghurst into Woolloomooloo, every building and IV tree glistening with anxiety, into the ground floor foyer of an apartment building. Then we were all in the elevator together. No one spoke much.

The doors opened on Zira's floor. Crimson carpet led us down a hall to double doors. Zira opened them up to reveal a wide space where the kitchen island counter flowed into the living room and dining room, all open plan. Tall, elegant IV pot plants bloomed red with flowers. Floor-to-ceiling windows offered a vast view of the city, twinkling.

Zira began pulling bottles and glasses out of cupboards, preparing drinks. Mikael went straight to the stereo, which was just a screen on a small stand that held all the music apps, invisibly linked to the tall speakers. I saw see him log in with the passcode.

"Do you live together, too?" I asked as I leaned against the island counter.

"No," they both said in unison. We all looked at each other, and smiled for the first time since leaving the venue.

"We spend enough time together, though," said Zira.

Mikael took my hand in his and gently pulled me toward the living space, near the windows. His pout was sorrowful, but he looked me in the eyes, spun me around, slowly, dancing with me, swaying. It felt good to be with him. I wanted Zira, too, but Mikael felt like a gateway, a facilitator, a comfort. A man, feminine. We stopped and just held each other. His head disappeared down toward my shoulder. I felt his breath tickle my neck. His lips grazed my skin, leaving a trail of phantom sensations along my collarbone and slowly up around my throat. I forgot to breathe. I wanted ...

"I'm glad we're all ok, anyway," said Zira. "Those absolute cunts."

Mikael and I parted. Zira sat on the huge couch that faced the city. On the marble coffee table in front of her were three brown cocktails and a framed painting with a glass front, facing up, depicting two demons copulating. There was a pile of powder on it, a $50 note rolled up as a thin tube, held together by the filter of a cigarette, and three lines laid out next to it, two bigger than the other. Next to all this was a bowl full of the devil's lettuce, the marijuana. Over this bowl, Zira was rolling up a joint.

"Those absolute ... Mikael, Cristi! Come over here."

We approached and all sat on the couch.

"I mean, I'm ... we're professionals, we're good people in society. It's just that we like to get loose, too. I'm still at the office on time. I work hard. I just love getting fucked up, too."

She licked along the paper of the joint, tucked, rolled, and twisted the tip to finish. She lit up and I saw Bacch in her face, the same focus, the same relief on the exhale. Not the same smile, but still. She passed to me. I tried it, passed it to Mikael. We cheers'd with the drinks, and turned to look out the giant windows overlooking the giant city. The Domain parklands were somewhere below, leaving the view unobstructed. The city sparkled. Zira pointed out the gap in the skyline where the casino used to be.

"Did you lose someone that day?"

Myself. But I said nothing.

Zira put her free arm around me, and we looked at that blank space in the city sky. I wondered about Bacch, where he was out there. I wondered about myself, why I was up here. I nestled in to Zira. She turned to face me. I didn't understand how eyes could be so comforting and daring at the same time. Her face had earned lines and wrinkles in her life but that only made her more of a glowing goddess. She put her fingers through my hair, tucking some behind my ear.

"You're too good, sweet Cristina."

I surrendered. I felt tied to a billion balloons, letting myself go in the ebb and flow of hopelessness. I leaned in, but instead of her lips, I let my mouth hover just close enough to the skin on her shoulder, like Mikael did, before dropping what I hoped were gentle kisses along her collarbone and slowly, slowly, up her neck. I could see she had goose bumps. *Did I cause that?* She stretched her neck up so that her head was titled back. I reached her chin. Our lips were already wet despite the smoke and we collapsed together into a state of unrestraint.

No wonder people sin when it feels like this.

For a moment I floundered in the awkward realisation that I had no idea what I was doing, especially as I began to feel three hands massaging me and pulling me in. My heartbeat went wild. I groped for Zira with one hand, Mikael with the other.

"Are you comfortable with this?" asked Zira between mouthfuls.

"Yes. But are we still going to that party?"

"We're already here."

The entire skyline sprawled out before us, watching us.

"Cristina, do you ever touch yourself?" asked Zira.

"No."

"Why not?"

"I feel ... guilty, like it's not right for some reason."

"Didn't you say everything wrong was right," said Mikael, "and right, wrong?"

"Do you want to touch yourself now?" asked Zira.

I was afraid and I didn't know what to do.

Not afraid of them. Afraid of myself. I wasn't prepared for this. These people were too open. I remembered being outside back home, skin in the summer moonlight, the warm wind and my own fingers, full of fear.

"Yes," I whispered. "I want to."

Colour burst from the corner of my eye, where bright waratah flowers began growing out of the far wall.

Zira and Mikael kissed each other, as if they knew just how to play the other, slow, strong, light, off the lips and across the body. I let my hand drift beneath my own dress, already wet, but hesitant. My fragile teasing only heightened it all and these two kept getting hotter and heavier in front of me and I got hotter and heavier with myself and God

I never knew you could feel so many things at once ... Zira and Mikael noticed. They looked at each other, then back at me.

What were they going to do to me?

Mikael got on his knees, hitched up my dress and slowly kissed up along my thighs. Zira was still kissing me and I was rubbing myself hopelessly and finally Mikael's mouth got there, but all he did was suckle on my fingers and then kissed along my other thigh, even slower, and I went faster, lost, finally found.

Giant king ferns were rising up and engulfing us there in the apartment, fan palms bursting up through everything and when he finally reached my pussy – I don't like using that word, but I just don't know better terms here – it felt like I was about to go over a waterfall. All that mouth and tongue and warm rainforest wetness, right where you open up to the world. Vines burst through walls and pipes and roots gripping tight. I could feel myself about to hit blissful oblivion when I felt my legs spread even wider and while Zira was still on the couch she leaned down over me and her mouth and tongue and lips joined Mikael's mouth and tongue and lips and my entire body shuddered as if every particle inside me had been violently lit up, shining like a galaxy of unknown pleasure, beautiful bodies there lapping it all up. The waratahs bloomed, as if opened up by force. Rainforest water welled on plants before becoming too heavy on leaves, leaving them to heave and overflow and drip everywhere. Who knows how long it lasted.

When I finally managed to open my eyes again, the city looked back at me without emotion. I felt weak. Zira and Mikael were grinning and wiping each other's faces and chins. The wild growth all around us slowed, stopped, suspended.

Mikael kissed me and I could taste myself on his lips. It wasn't bad. Kind of hot, just how raw and unglamorous and human it was. Zira disappeared. My head was still dizzy, filled to the brim, overflowing. I pulled my dress back down as Mikael rolled off and positioned himself next to the coffee table. Zira returned and I barely realised what they were doing, still coming down from whatever blooming heaven I had been beamed up to, interplanetary puppeteers pulling strings I'd needed pulled, until they passed me the rolled-up note and offered the small line.

"Would you like some, Cristina?" asked Zira, sinking down on my right side, Mikael on my left.

"Um …"

"It's not much. Just enough. Too much can interfere …"

"Have you done it before?" asked Mikael, playing with his nose, still sniffing.

"No."

"Only if you want," said Zira. She began nibbling at my earlobe.

I took the rolled note without thinking, bent over the glass painting of the demons and vacuumed the remaining line, messing it up and leaving bits behind. Mikael wiped up my leftovers with a fingertip. He held it at my mouth to suck on. I obliged. I wrapped my lips around his finger. I could feel him massaging my gums, until I couldn't feel my gums anymore. Your body knew it was chemical. It crawled through you.

They offered me a glass of water. They sucked back theirs and I realised how thirsty I was.

"Thank you."

"Prove it," said Zira.

"What?"

"Prove you're thankful."

Well, I slid off the couch to kneel in front of Zira. That black dress that had criss-crossed her legs all night was now tugged to the side and finally nothing separated me from her. Tangled wildflowers grew up from behind the couch and down the cushions. I kissed her like Mikael had kissed my thighs. He'd pulled on a condom and moved behind me.

He whispered in my ear, "Do you want this?"

I nodded, and some of my hair brushed Zira. Her legs quivered.

"Yes, please …"

I felt Mikael behind me. It slid and slid and then …

Jesus Christ.

He took me while I took her. Her hand gripped my hair and pushed me even deeper inside her as Mikael pushed deeper inside me and I had never ever known anything like this.

I felt degraded and worshipped at the same time.

Apple trees erupted down through the roof, cracking the ceiling, their fruits hanging heavy and low and already ripe. Mikael kissed along my back and shoulders as he continued his strides inside me. Zira would look down at me across the mounds and valleys of her body, her eyes screaming that there was nothing she needed more in this world than me, right there and then. I wanted to come so so badly, but something was blocking that final push. Was it the cocaine? *What have I done?* Zira gripped my hair at the scalp, yelping. Mikael became more determined. He hit nerve endings I'd never thought I had, never dreamed they could experience such transcendental insanity until I thought I might finally spill over the edge, *please please please*, like Mikael pulling fruit from the branch but straining to pluck it, the stem resisting but the pull getting fiercer, desperate. A horrible piercing siren alarm cut through everything, just as I felt the giant cosmic rock of Jesus's tomb finally shift to reveal the divine resurrection, the apple about to yield to the tug, and the alarm rang on and on, far too loudly, a robotic male voice saying:

"EVACUATE NOW, YOUR BUILDING IS ON FIRE, PLEASE EVACUATE NOW, OR YOU MIGHT DIE, EJACULATE NOW, OR YOU MIGHT DIE, EVACUATE OR BURN TO DEATH, WHY DOES NO ONE EVER TAKE ME SERIOUSLY, THIS IS NOT A DRILL, A DRILLING, NOT JUST BURNT TOAST THIS TIME, PLEASE EJACULATE, YOU HAVE TO ESCAPE, NOW, YES, GIRL, ALMOST ..."

"Oh my god are you fucking kidding me ..." screamed Zira as her entire body convulsed, but the fire alarm kept screaming at us. The boulder was blocking the tomb again and I couldn't get back to that edge, couldn't pluck the apple, left hanging from the vine. Mikael stopped

moving inside me and Zira stopped moving. I was kneeling there with a dick going limp inside me, a face covered in a woman's come, and the fire alarm still screaming, *"PLEASE EVACUATE NOW, YOUR BUILDING IS ON FUCKING FIRE, IS ANYONE LISTENING TO ME? EVACUATE NOW, WHAT IF IT'S NOT JUST BURNT TOAST THIS ONE TIME ... EJACULATE NOW ... I MEAN IT PROBABLY IS JUST BURNT TOAST BUT STILL ..."*

"Oh god, let's just go downstairs," yelled Zira over the noise. Mikael moved off and out of me. My muscles all contracted. He helped me stand up. I wrapped myself up in my dress, my damp underwear, pulling myself back together. Zira disappeared. Mikael removed the condom – he hadn't come. He noticed me noticing it.

Zira reappeared wearing a huge white fur dressing gown and not much else. She topped up the drinks while the alarm continued screaming. She cut lines again, using one of her business cards. I joined them, going last. I pocketed the card. We moved to leave, to escape the alarm, my clitoris still swollen and hot and hoping.

Looking around the apartment as we left, there was no wild flora, no tree branches, no structural damage, no waratahs or palm fronds. Just the vast windows and the sparkling, grinning, winking city.

We had to take the fire stairs. We spilled the drinks a bit but made it down to see a fire truck and a crowd of half-dressed residents and their families, their lovers, their pets, their cigarettes, standing or sitting on the ground, on their phones. The firemen said it was just burnt toast, a false alarm, but they had to do their due diligence according to Org safety regulations, especially now, after the casino. Mikael and Zira's eyes were huge in the flashing blue and red lights. Mine must have been, too.

"How are you feeling, sweet Cristina?" She opened her arms and I snuggled into her embrace, my veins strung high and wanting her touch. There was plenty of skin beneath her coat to touch.

She whipped out a pack of cigarettes. Rotting human organs covered the packet. She offered me one. I almost said yes, craving something to rattle through my lungs with more weight than mere air, but I stopped myself. They lit up, whispering, watching the firemen.

I walked away a little. No shoes, warm night, cold feet. I looked up at the polluted sky, unable to see any stars. After a while I looked back to see Mikael and Zira straddling a fireman each, up against the other side of the truck. They were really going at it. My shoes were still upstairs but I wanted to run. Was it the cocaine? Is this how some people live? *Is this how I live?* It hadn't been such a bad night. Quite the contrary. Quite the night.

I could see Zira now dancing in the street while Mikael and the two firemen watched, her full fur figure illuminated, on and off, by the red and blue strobe lights.

I bolted into the night, hoping Bacch was home. The city at night. I laughed hysterically at myself, at the world. Empty streets welcomed me with silent nonchalance. Magic is everywhere. Alleyways are sanctuaries. But then I passed a man leaning against a wall and he began following me. I ran harder and he disappeared behind me because I was flying. I was fucking flying. No one teaches you about these moments. No preparation. You just have to stumble upon life yourself. But I slowed down because I could feel cuts in my feet and I could barely breathe. At William Street, I got in a taxi and gave the address. The driver said I looked beautiful and suggested I go to his place instead. I jumped out at a set of red lights in Surry Hills without paying and ran off between buildings until I finally got to the apartment, fumbled with the keys and walked upstairs with a headache I'd never felt before.

Bacch was home and asleep. I vomited in the toilet and lay on the couch with the stereo on low, crying now and then, drinking water from a jug, barely noticing the spillage. Fitful. Awake. I wanted to crawl into bed with Bacch, but I was too ashamed. There were bags and bags of sugary baked goods crammed inside the tiny apartment and I didn't know why. I eventually went to my bed. All my muscles felt like restless, starving snakes trying to escape my own skin.

Bacch

What a beautiful day! The Saturday morning sun lit up the apartment like I'd rarely seen it. Perhaps because I'd rarely seen morning sun. I showered & shaved. I looked up city rentals. Jazztronica on the stereo. I did some push-ups between the bread bags. Tried to be responsible. At least for a day. Only seven nights left. Should make the most of it.

I heard Cristi's door slowly crack open. She had never ever slept later than me. Staff drinks gone wild, perhaps. Her footsteps were always soft yet firm – you get to know such things in close quarters – but not today.

She appeared around the corner, robe wrapped around her, shoulders hunched, eyes half closed, loose in their sockets, like mine most mornings. She shuffled between the overflowing sugary bags & sat in the chair across from me.

"Good morning," I chirped.

She just looked at me.

"Are you ok?"

"Please ..." She swallowed, trying to clear the rust in her throat. "Tea ..."

I stood to boil the kettle. "Where were you last night?"

She didn't reply.

"Do you want any food? There's plenty here."

She managed to ask about all the bakery goods & I explained my new business venture.

"That's one of the most ... most preposterous things I've ever heard," she said.

"Do you wanna help sell some?"

She went to the bathroom & vomited.

I finished brewing her lemon & ginger tea, cut up some fruits, put leftover pizza in the oven, lit the incense, readied some Disney film on the laptop & prepared the soft blankets on the couch for what I imagined was Cristi's first hangover.

She said she needed painkillers, but we didn't have any. I offered a joint but she said the last thing she needed was more drugs. I lit up anyway. She took a small puff, and a bigger one a few moments later. She was in bed before dinner.

Sleep didn't come to me so easily, so I went walking, found some cheap takeaway dinner, kept walking the streets, hoping something might happen – but it never did & I went back to the apartment. Moss had begun growing on the front door.

I called Hari. He actually answered.

In no time, I was at a headland doof.

In the Uber, by myself, I opened a bottle of wine I'd grabbed. I'd started keeping the red in the fridge, otherwise it was just too hot. I drank it in. All of it.

"What's out here, mate?" asked the driver.

"Emptiness."

He didn't ask any more questions.

Probably seemed dramatic, but it was risky to reveal the doof, in case it got reported to the Protectors. This was a one-nighter near the city, hopefully an all-nighter, though we take what we can get. Normally a doof went for days & nights, non-stop music, everyone camped deep in the bush, too far for Ubers & taxis & Protectors, all of us dressed up or dressed down, art & coloured lights on trees, the galaxy glistening & exposed above.

The car reached the end of the road. I hopped out to see Hari & some of his crew. We were on a headland off southern Sydney somewhere. Breezy scrub. Above, the stars struggled to peek through the orange glow of city haze. I threw the empty bottle into a lone garbage bin, no recycling bins, before a bit of a trek down dark bush tracks, using lights from our phones to find our way. Somewhere around here, the organisers would have set up cameras, in case the Protectors showed up.

Memorise the ways in & out, in case you need a fast getaway.

And then the first thing you hear, above the whispers of the wind & yourselves, is the four-to-the-floor bass of the kick.

doof doof doof doof doof doof doof doof

That's when you know you've made it, when it's a secret location, when you get a riddle or a last-minute address pop up on your phone.

doof doof doof doof-d-doof doof doof doof-d-doof

Yeah so that's why it's called a doof.

The wind was fresh & salty. Tucked into a hill, facing out to sea, hanging off the edge of the coast in the darkness, was a reinforced concrete bunker, some abandoned military post. I couldn't quite tell; it was being used very differently to its original intention. Lights flashed from within, like the mouth of a cosmic tiger head, the entrance to the Cave of Wonders. People were everywhere, silhouettes dancing, briefly detailed by multicoloured flashes. Some in wild outfits, others dressed casually, just bopping around with friends. The edge of the earth dropped off metres away in the darkness, while we celebrated & escaped & tried to love each other & ourselves.

Hari pulled me into the crowd, towards the DJ booth. To get there, we had to go deeper into the bunker, to the back of the throat. But people parted easily, swaying, happy to groove with you for a passing moment. There were some super cooked units, eyes staring out their ears, rubbing their sweating selves, in their own worlds. But most were cruising & bouncing, checking it all out, digging it, big pupils & bigger smiles.

doof doof doof doof-d-doof doof doof doof-d-doof

We reached the back of the throat, which was the front of the dancefloor. They had hectic speakers set up. The sound was off its head. If we got busted, you'd wanna have a plan to save the gear from within this cornered space. Hari said hi to the DJ as I followed, stepping through people. The moving lights disoriented you in the darkness. Hari passed me a cap. I took it, dry swallowed.

It had been such a healthy start to the day.

And there was a girl dancing there, where we were, facing out across the crowd from behind the DJ booth. She seemed familiar. The girl with the gap teeth from that warehouse party. *Winnie?*

The cap caught in my throat for a moment. Tears appeared at my eyes as my tongue pushed saliva down the back of my Cave of Wonders & I managed to choke & swallow.

The girl noticed me, and smiled, and I smiled & wiped my face as the kick drums disappeared & a deep synth stab picked up. Hari grabbed me.

"I fuckin *love* this tune," he screamed. "*Listen*, Jacques Greene and, and Cadence Weapon, I think. Hectic shit. Geniuses. *Welcome, bruddaaaaa.*"

I had called him late, but I was right on time for these nocturnal humans. Hari introduced me to the guy next to Winnie.

"Giao," said the guy, then motioned to the girl. "My cousin."

We introduced ourselves again, sly smiles hinting at our familiarity. I was wrong. Her name was Wendy, not Winnie. Her outfit wasn't quite so wild as before – slim-fit trackies & a colourful windbreaker. Hari immediately interrupted.

"Get *amongst* this shit, *LISTEN*..."

And so we listened & danced & looked & felt & tasted all in the flashing sweating darkness, where people moved, where people were moved, where the Wonders were, where we were. We were swimming in the sesh. The sea roared somewhere below. The sermon had begun.

Through cerulean hue
Praise place comes into view
Chants fill up the room
Strange sounds underneath the moon
Hands raised to the roof
Grey slate under black boots
Best friend you never knew
Miracles coming out the blue
Circle dance like a Quaker
Brings me right back to the pit
Eyes search for a saviour
Never know when this is it
Preaching to the congregation
Club burning up, conflagration
Bread & wine, consecrated
Let's have a conversation
At night service
Saturday mass
Night service
Saturday mass
All the nights with stained glass
In the future see the past
Night service
Saturday mass

You look at everyone & marvel at it. Human beings just moving to the rhythms of invisible sound waves. We make it so beautiful. Imagine, some ancient beat our ancestors danced to together, around their lights, their fire, their clear & unadulterated stars. Here we are. Dancing in a concrete bunker, under threat of prosecution.

At some point a bunch of us left to smoke & see the place from outside. Hari, Wendy, Giao & I bustled through the crowd to the outskirts & walked around and up. You could sit on top of the bunker, legs dangling off the edge, looking out across an endless horizon, vast clouds, lit by the city, sending that orange light to dance faintly atop the sea. Headlands stretched north & south into misty blackness. It wasn't sunset, and thankfully I wasn't drinking goon, but I spared a moment for Kafi & his dreams of freedom. And what of Ria's dreams of freedom? What of so many human beings' freedoms?

"I think I met you at that church warehouse sesh," Giao was saying.

Hari & Giao were rolling darts above their baccy pouches. I took a lighter & a mint tin from my pocket, popped the lid. Out slid my joint. Wendy just looked out across the sea & sipped her water bottle.

"Yeah, we met briefly," I said to Giao, lighting up the tip. "You dance well, I remember."

Giao chuckled as he popped the rollie in his mouth. "You danced with Wendy, I remember."

We all wore smiles of mischief. Except Hari. Hari's rollie dangled from his mouth, the strings of tobacco poking out the end of the lil white tube. He was looking at his phone.

"What's wrong?" I said after an exhale. I felt the cap tickling my muscles, the first ripples running through my body, the ocean air lifting us higher atop the headland bunker.

Breathe in, deeply.

Breathe out, deeply.

doof doof doof doof-d-doof doof doof doof-d-doof

"I need to leave," Hari whispered in my ear. His eyes were glassy, but maybe that was just the gear.

"Is everything ok?" I asked him, also in a whisper, while Giao & Wendy chatted. "Your mum? Your cousin?"

"A client ..."

"Brudda, you only just got here. Tell him to wait a day."

"I normally would." He pressed his palms into his temples. "This is my time, brudda, my holiday, for a night. But this ... this is one you just don't say no to."

"A Servant?"

But Hari was already saying goodbye to Giao & Wendy. We all stood up & hugged. I offered to walk him back, but he said not to worry, enjoy the party, he'd prefer to go alone, but of course he'd prefer to stay. He turned his back to us & the wind, lit the rollie, exhaled, and walked off into the darkness, back to civilisation.

The come up was hitting me hard. The wine sloshed in my stomach. With Hari's departure, my heart was a mongrel baby animal, crying & screaming. I felt stranded on this strange bunker, surrounded by black waters. I wanted to be home & snuggled up with other warm loving bodies, with Hari, with Cristi, safe, maybe some hidden sanctuary in this ancient land, somewhere that The Org doesn't know about or think it owns.

"Are you ok?" Wendy asked.

Giao stood staring after Hari with a strange look. "I really wanted to fuck him tonight," he said, shaking his head.

"I was asking you," she said, putting her hand on my forearm, gently touching, like the light atop the sea that spread before us.

"I dunno," I said, looking at the splotches of grass & dirt & gravel at my feet. "I dunno."

"Fuck this," said Giao. "Let's dance."

We began descending. I offered the j, Giao accepted, Wendy waved it away.

"We get random drug tests," she said. "I'm happy just to have a late coffee & dance."

"You seemed super on it when we met."

"It was my birthday, my first & only time." We went down single file, Wendy & I holding hands, for support, until we were near the mouth of the bunker. "Giao asked if I wanted to go to a party. I was stressed out.

The new job had been tense. I'd never really been out with him. It was very different. I would never dress like that normally."

"I think that's the point. Dress how you'd never dress normally."

Giao passed me back the j & slid into the crowd. Wendy & I stayed further out, bopping along, where there was more space between people. 'I Get Deep' was in full swing, a remix, deep jackin bass, Roland Clark on the rhythmic vocal.

> *Raising both hands in the air as if Jesus was a DJ himself*
> *Spinnin those funky funky funky house beats*
> *And in this temple we all pray in unity for the same things*

A guy & a girl were having some wild interpretative dance-off. A young camp fella drifted past us. Purple lipstick. Hair cut as short as his short shorts.

"Are you bitches *sell*ing?"

We disappointed him. He boogied off with a wink.

"They're getting stricter with that stuff at work," she said, watching the crowd. "People talking about it more often, getting tested more often."

"Where do you work?"

"The Org. The Youth Program."

I felt upheavals. The air was sticky. The world had taken on a new lens. Hot waves rolled inside me. It felt so fucking good. Here we go. But, if I go too deep, I might not want to speak much, and when I do it has to be something meaningful, something deep, something deep & meaningful.

The Org?

"Wait, what?" I said, as if in a dream. "I didn't think you'd ... be from The Org ... doing ... these things."

"Thank Giao."

"Thanks, Giao."

132

"I mean I'm not making it a habit," she continued. "But the world is burning & I just need to get out of it sometimes. I know that makes me weak, a sinner, but that's how it is."

"Nothing about that is weak or sinful," I said, turning to look at her glowing face. "We don't live in an environment that meets our basic human needs. So, we do what we can."

"And I thought The Org met all our needs, ever since the last pandemic."

The world was too wobbly. I was too high for this conversation.

"Do you salsa?" she asked.

"Um ... nah ..."

"I do," said some nearby hunk in a faux-leopard onesie.

Wendy took his hand & was suddenly swept up in movement with old mate. I felt nothing but warmth for both of them. Jealousy is useless. Compersion – the joy in someone else's joy – is the opposite. It feels a lot better than clinging to some negative illusion about your self worth. Rejection and acceptance are equally unhelpful. Both hinge your sense of self, of reality, to the unreliable & conflicting ebb & flow of others.

Besides, they moved with such flair, such ebb & flow. Why extinguish beauty? I'd been to some latin nights before, but not enough to dance salsa like that. But it didn't matter. My insides had taken up the salsa spins as well. Twirls & flips & those upheavals. The tunes were getting heavier. Roland Clark's voice carried on through the mix. The wine was not going to stay down.

But the music gets me high
Sanctified like an old lady in church
We get happy
We stomp our feet
We clap our hands
We shout
We cry

133

We dance
And we say
Sweet Lord, speak to me
Speak to me, speak to me, speak to me
Because we love house music
And on this night it brings us together
Like a family reunion every week
We eat
We drink
We laugh
We play
We stink
So for all you hip hoppers
You doowoppers
Name droppers
You pill poppers
Come into our house
To get deep
Whaaa
To get deep ...

I tried to tap Wendy, but it was difficult to catch them, swirling around as much as they were. I got her attention briefly with my finger up, like, *I'll be right back*. Ah, little did I know what the Cave of Wonders had in store.

I ran out into the dark scrub, far enough from the madness to be hidden, and vomited up over half the bottle of wine. No sign of a half-digested capsule. I vomited more dark red gut liquid & hated myself for it. The knees of my jeans were deep in the dirt. My eyes were teary & bloodshot, my throat still coughing for a while. I spat a few times & rolled over to sit on the ground, forehead on my knees.

C'mon, Bacch, baby. Baby Bacch. Baby Back Ribs. Primates drowning their consciousness on a rock spinning around a star spinning around stars spinning around spinning around ah shit –

I vomited a bit more.

doof doof doof doof-d-doof doof doof doof-d-doof

I wanted to gouge the loneliness out of my ribcage.

doof doof doof doof-d-doof doof doof doof-d-doof

Then, the worst disco lights ever. Red & blue. In the distance, through the tree line, the flashing lights of Protector vehicles, no sirens. They seemed to have pulled up where I'd been dropped off, where the road ended & the dirt tracks began. There was movement. They were all getting out.

There was nothing else nearby. They could only be coming for us. Wendy. Giao. Everyone. The speakers. The music. The freedom.

I started running to warn them, but tripped. Of course I tripped. The music cut out. One of the organisers must have already seen the Protectors on their camera surveillance. The yelling began. People started grabbing people & running, bolting, many towards me. I couldn't tell where Wendy or Giao was. The lights cut out. The Cave of Wonders, extinguished. Just overgrown stone & graffiti-covered concrete.

More people were running past me. Protectors were coming for us. I took a deep breath, in, oooh, out, oooh. I was rolling fucking hard on the molly baby. Everything, so big, so wild, and the sea still sang somewhere below. Leopard hunk busted past in a dark rush of bodies. Like a lost lil fishy, I jumped in with them & swam my heart out. To survive.

Drugs can enhance pleasure to insane degrees, but they can also exacerbate inescapable terrors. I don't remember much other than blindly running & my heart thumping so hard in my strained chest that I thought I might be on the verge of a cardiac episode. At some point I came near some of the advancing Protectors. I threw myself to the ground behind a cluster of spinifex & other bush, tried to become the dirt. I stayed there for who knows how long. Screams came from back near the bunker. I was close to the road though. Those red & blue disco lights flashed nearby. Eventually I peeked out. Leopard hunk was handcuffed, teeth bared, roaring, shoved into the Protector van. Extinguished. Disappeared.

More figures moved near me. I became the dirt again.

I felt hunted, my arteries, veins, the blood running through me, in & out of that boxing fist of a heart ...

doof doof doof doof-d-doof doof doof doof-d-doof

I felt things moving around me. Was the spinifex growth thickening? Was the bush growing, in front of me? Or was it just my mixed up neurochemistry? Where were Wendy & Giao? Where was Hari? Ria? Bianca?

Cristi?

Cristi

I woke up to go to the bathroom, but I hadn't had dinner. Bacch's door was open. He wasn't home. Saturday night. Along with the excessive bakery goods, he'd left a half-full takeaway container of food in the fridge. I microwaved and ate that. He owed me. I promised myself that I'd ask him about the eviction in the morning, or whenever he'd be back. I took a pink donut as dessert.

When I eventually dozed off, I dreamt I was on that strange infinite beach of my youth, where waves lapped the clouds and stars shone in the sand. The lifeguard wasn't there, but Bacch was. He was curled up in the shimmering dunes. I approached and laid down with him. We were naked. We embraced. Fingers interlocked. Bodies intertwined. Strands of dune grasses and creepers grew around us, creating a natural cocoon. The sea sang somewhere beyond us.

Such moments of perfection shatter too quickly, in dreams and life.

Hands hacked at the scrub, tore us apart. Protectors had found us. We were on a headland now, and Bacch was being dragged away through the spinifex toward flashing vans, screaming. Ahead of him, they were trying to shove a huge live leopard into the back, chained and roaring to the sky. Wendy and Hari were there too, standing there, watching.

Before I could contemplate such appearances, I was dragged off by my hair and arms, still naked, by multiple Protectors. But they dragged me in the other direction. I kicked and kicked and dry dust plumed up in the vivid night. The vans, the leopard, Wendy, Bacch, they all got smaller and further away until the dust and darkness swallowed them.

I thrashed and thrashed. My scalp was being torn from my skull. The hands held strong.

How can you not try to resist this?

It was just us, the land, the sky, and the sea. The earth was moving. Constantly, but I saw it especially now, all the little ecosystems and biological networks pulsing and surviving throughout the land. Crown land. I was not alone. The earth tried to cradle me again, like on the beach. A sense of longing overwhelmed me, almost entirely taking over the sense of physical struggle with my captors. The land was me.

I wasn't a sinner. I wasn't a robot. I was not even an independent being. I was made up of the same stuff everything else is, everyone else. The land embraced me, but I was still kicking. The land could not promise comfort or judgement or reason. She is life, but She is also death. She is harsh, but She is bountiful.

He is wrath, but He is mercy.

I still couldn't see the Protectors dragging me. My hands gripped their uniformed forearms, trying to keep some slack so my head wouldn't tear from my body. The land whispered. It lives. It moves. It was obvious. The Org was an occupying force. The King, the Protectors and the Servants were an occupying force. The land weeps. Do we? Everything began to spin. The Protectors threw me off the headland. Through the endless air. The sea sang somewhere below. I woke up whimpering and thrashing in my sweat-soaked sheets. Still falling.

I went to get water.

Bacch still wasn't home.

Just a dream.

Bacch

I lay there, curled up, tucked away below a scrubby patch of bush, for who knows how long. A baby on the gear, in a womb of dirt & spinifex & wine & vomit-stained clothing. *Would they find me? Would they find Wendy?* I stayed down. I stayed down. Time stretched. Several moments occurred in which I thought they'd found me, but somehow the torch light just missed. I wondered if The Org had given them night vision goggles for busting up parties.

Is this how to survive the 21ˢᵗ century? Just hide?

After a long absence of noise or light, I snuck a peek. The vans were gone. I still stayed down for a while, just trying to breathe normally.

I didn't want to order an Uber from here, in case Protectors were tracking app data to identify attendees. When your government behaves like this, paranoia becomes palpable, even necessary. So, I walked. I limped. It felt like I'd had strips torn from inside me. I wondered what had happened to everyone. Were people still hiding in the bushes around me?

I walked until suburban houses popped up, a safe enough distance. I sat on the gutter and ordered my ride.

MDMA can help loosen your grip on your ego & let you just experience love & joy, generally & universally, in empathetic connection to everyone & everything. But now, I only felt fear & distress & utter exhaustion, like my skeleton had slashed its way through my body & escaped, leaving me to pick up the pieces.

Wendy & I never even got to exchange details.

I should learn how to salsa.

I should do a lot of things.

The Uber appeared after a while. I got in the front seat, *how's your night going mate*, and put the radio to FBi 94.5 FM. They were playing emotional club tunes. We drove off. I danced in my seat. Even got the driver bopping for a bit there. All the energy & revelry I'd hoped to indulge in throughout the evening, it came out in that passenger seat, the seatbelt straining to contain my limbs.

I got away. I got away. I'm away, baby. Baby Bacch. Baby ...

The driver stopped bopping & just looked at me strangely from time to time. Eventually I stopped too, closed my eyes, and put my head in my hands, hair dangling everywhere.

We pulled up. I got out. No street lights. As the car drove off, I looked around. I hadn't even noticed that we'd gone to Newtown. I'd put in the wrong address. How did I manage this? I stood out front of Bianca's apartment. She was probably snug in bed with her man. Happiness can be that simple. I was happy for her. I was sad for me. I tried not to be, but some things can't be helped.

This is not my beautiful house. This is not my beautiful ... whatever we were.

I couldn't afford all these Ubers, so I walked to Newtown station to head to Central, the heart of the beast, my lil spot in the sky with Cristi. My skull pounded in the morning quiet.

On the train home, I tried to look out the window, up at the world, but the bright lighting inside the carriage meant all I saw was my own reflection, transparent & ghostlike against the darkness outside. Forehead & cheeks & eye sockets rubbed & pressed against the glass as the comedown began to gnaw at my skin, my bones. Under prohibition, you never know what shit your gear is cut with. I thought back to rolling together with beautiful friends, on the sesh, looking out for each other, caring, knowing, loving, empathy shining, bodies grooving, hearts melting. Beautiful friends I didn't keep in touch with.

rattle rattle rattle

The sound of the carriages & wheels grated against my skull, the noise getting inside me. I took out my phone to put on a track, HNNY or Coltrane or anyone. Piano keys began, comforting me a little. I reactivated my dating apps, swiped through a few times, and then threw my phone at the fucking window. I picked it up. Cracked screen. No roses. It was useless. I was useless.

Connection through phones. Companionship in capsules.

Eventually I got home. Up the stairs. Opened the door. I looked at all the bakery leftovers in the living room.

What the fuck am I doing? This is not me. Have I let life slip through my fingers? How could Cristina ever love me like this? Who will ever love me? Who will ever employ me? I'm not an entrepreneur – stealing leftovers & hawking them doesn't nearly count. I am so small & meaningless in the grand evolutionary & cosmic chain & I don't have enough serotonin in my brain to convince myself otherwise. I am alone and my soul is dead, if ever I had one.

I fear this scrambled world, built by generations of other humans for us to scramble through. I fear advertising & screens, though I studied digital marketing. Did I study that? I fear I'll forget those years of my life. I fear that those were the best years of my life. I fear that I am inadequate. I fear that I will never reach my potential, or that I have no potential at all. I fear that I am all talk & no action. I fear that I'm walking down the wrong path in life. I fear I will not find fulfilment in my career, whatever it may be. I fear I won't find a career. I fear myself. I fear myself.

There are infinite lives you could live, yet you get one.

Cristi

I wanted to confront him in the morning, but he slept til the arvo, curled up with a summer sheet on the couch. Drained skin. Mouth open, tongue half out. Bruise across his forehead.

Had I looked that pitiful? Lying there like that all day? Lying ...

"Oi!"

Nothing.

I poked him a few times. Slapped his face a little. Still nothing.

I put on Powderfinger's *Odyssey Number Five*, cranked the stereo and paced the apartment, eviction notice in hand. He still hadn't woken up by the time 'My Happiness' finished. When 'The Metre' began, Bacch rolled over.

"Mmm, yrmmm ..."

I turned the stereo down and sat on the couch next to his bundled legs. "What?"

"Great album ..."

I tossed the letter at him. He scrambled to sit up. His face turned somehow more ashen. The sheet fell to the floor.

"Cristi, Cristina ..."

"What was your plan?"

"I'm sorry," he mumbled, rubbing his face. "I didn't have a plan."

"Maybe that's your problem," I said. "I thought we had a good thing going here."

"We *do*." He said it more like a plea than a statement.

I shook my head. "Now we have a week to find a new place to live. Or have you been doing inspections without me too?"

"No. I just ... couldn't bear the thought of you leaving me." He coughed, got to his feet and shuffled to the kitchen sink, stepping around the bags of baked goods. Tap on, mouth in the stream, as strong as possible with the low pressure up here.

I stayed on the couch. I didn't turn to face him. "I found your books, too."

"Why were you in my room?"

"I wanted to read. The Bible. Tell me why you cut it up."

He stayed in the kitchen.

"Tell me, Bacch. Please."

"Look, most nights, I have no one. Nothing to do. No offers for job interviews. Sometimes, occasionally, I read, cutting and pasting bits together to compare the Bible, the Quran, the Pāli Canon. Plus, they're a great texture for rolling papers when I run out."

"But *why*? Why do you have to do that?"

"That's how I have to learn, to understand," he said. "You follow your orders, but I have to know why the orders exist, what their justification is, especially when there are different orders, conflicting truths, to choose from. To study machinery, you pull it apart and rebuild it."

"These are holy books though. That matters to people. You must respect that?"

"Respect must be earned, not demanded."

I shook my head. "You're just angry. At religions. At Protectors. At The Org. At everything."

"Of course I am!" His hands gripped the edge of the kitchen counter, arms rigid, weight against it. "None of this is natural! None of it is justified! It's just doing what humans have always done – dominate, rule, manipulate. This is how Australia was founded, it's how the whole world was built, kings and subjects, and we wonder WHY things barely change. Give me one reason to respect any of them. People are being murdered, disappeared, thrown in cells, just for trying to live, to thrive, to follow their own path. Why is the onus on us? *Why is no one with power doing anything fucking responsible?"*

"Trust me," I said, very aware of the honesty I had withheld. Yes. I had to tell him the truth. "There are good people working at The Org trying to fix things, trying to make The Org better."

"FUCK THE ORG!"

There was loud, rapid knocking at the door. We fell silent. Street noise became audible. Very audible. Louder than usual, with yelling and honks and more knocks at the door. Bacch and I exchanged glances in the tension.

"Is anyone home?" It was a girl's voice.

Bacch ran into his room and closed the door.

"Bacch?" I called after him.

"Hello?" came the girl's voice.

"One second!" I said.

I unlocked and opened the door. It was an Org Scout, bright as a button, the plaid skirt, the red white and blue, the lipstick, the basket, lid closed.

"Oh, hello," she said. "Do you live here?"

"I do. How can I help?"

She looked past me, scanning the apartment. Her wide eyes found the big painting, the koala on the cross in a bushfire. "We've heard from one of your neighbours that you have books worth donating to the burn."

"I haven't heard of any burn?"

"It hasn't been widely publicised," said the Scout. "You wouldn't know about it."

I checked behind me. Bacch was still in his room. I whispered, "I work at The Org. In publicity. Why not announce this?"

"National security," she shrugged. "Didn't want to spoil the surprise. Not that we haven't been here before. I met your ... housemate."

"You've been here before?"

"Are you going to hand over the books?"

"What books?"

The Scout sighed, and stepped back. "I'm sorry, you seem real nice, but we still have a few more blocks to go today."

She pulled a mobile from her basket as Bacch emerged and approached. She smiled when she saw him. I looked at him. He'd never looked worse. Embellished dishevelment.

"Hello again!" she said.

"Oh, hi," he said.

"This is your last chance."

"What?"

"Anything you think could be contraband, bring it out now." She walked past me into the living room, past Bacch's cactus plant. "Contraband could be anywhere."

"I told you," said Bacch. "I have nothing more to give to The Org."

She stepped over to him. A dreamlike intruder, in that ridiculous outfit. They stared at each other.

"Hey!" I said. "This is a *Sunday!* Get out of our home!"

The Scout's head snapped towards me, pigtails whipping around. Those wide eyes narrowed. She tapped the mobile screen a few times, before dropping it back in the basket and bringing out something else. A book. A white Bible. The Org's Bible. She placed it on the coffee table. Then she just walked out, saying along the way, "God bless The Org. God bless Australia. God bless Freedom."

Bacch and I shared a few moments of bewilderment. I closed and locked the door. We went to the balcony. The roads below were covered in Protectors. Heavy riot gear. People were streaming through the streets, hordes of humans, most moving to or from Prince Alfred Park. Before we could get a proper look, more fists banged on our front door.

"Who is it?"

They just kept banging. I looked at Bacch. He looked at the huge painting on the wall. The koala in the tree, on the cross, in the fire.

"Fuck ..." he said, and walked to the door. Opened it.

It all happened so fast.

Three Protectors pushed past into the apartment and began searching. They told us to sit on the couch and wait, unless we wanted to be strip searched. We sat on the couch and waited. The koala burned above us on the cross as the Protectors stormed the place. They pulled down the painting and walked out with it, along with all the bags of breads and donuts, all of the books, not even bothering to look through Bacch's chopped up holy books, and finally all of our pot plants. But they left the pots and instead just grabbed the plants themselves, torn out, uprooted, leaves and soil falling from their gloves across the floor, trailing out the door and down the stairs.

"C'mon, man," said Bacch, standing up as they left. "The plants too? The cactus?"

They walked out, but three more walked in. One came over to me, another stood in front of Bacch. The third said, "Empty your pockets."

I only had my phone. The Protector took it, threw it on the ground, next to the coffee table. Bacch only had the eviction notice. Tossed aside.

The third Protector spoke again. "Do you consent to being strip searched?"

"No," said Bacch. "We don't consent to any of this."

"That has been noted, but you must comply. Begin the strip searches."

I dread remembering this. My hands tremble. But you relive it every time you see it caught on film, or in a news article, or even just when you see a Protector in the street, walking past you, driving by. Inherent impunity.

My brother.

The Protectors pushed Bacch into the kitchen, and me toward the far corner of the living room, as far away from each other as possible. One Protector dealt with me, the other two dealt with Bacch. My Protector pressed something in the side of the helmet. The visor disappeared. There was a woman beneath the uniform.

"Take off your clothes. Quickly."

"Why?" I whimpered. I couldn't help but whimper. And surely if I seemed vulnerable, no threat, a decent human being, then they wouldn't push it, wouldn't arrest me, wouldn't make me take my clothes off.

"We're not leaving until the inspection is over."

I looked at her eyes. "I don't have a bra on."

"Take everything off. Everything."

How is this happening to me?

Everyone is a potential criminal.

I took off my shirt. Gave it to the Protector. She handled it, looked at it, threw it on the ground with my phone. I crossed my arms to cover my breasts. I could hear the Protectors getting louder and more aggressive with Bacch.

"Pull back your foreskin," they said.

"Please, no ..." I heard him say.

"What's wrong? If you've got nothing to hide, why don't you just cooperate?"

I started to cry.

"Don't cry," said the Protector in front of me. "Why are you crying?"

Isn't it obvious? But I couldn't say a word. I slowly pulled my shorts down my legs, stepped out of them, gave them to the Protector. Inspected. Discarded.

"Almost there," said the Protector. "You're doing great."

Are we friends now? My supporter? My mother? My Protector?

My brother? Is this what he's training for?

Tears. My body moved without my mind. My thumbs hooked in between my undies and my waist. My back bent over. My arms pulled my undies down. Legs stepped out of them. Offered them to the Protector but she waved them away. Hands tossed them on the coffee table.

Naked, except for the small cross that hung from my neck. One arm wrapped around my torso, trying to shield my breasts, trying to hug myself. My other hand covered my ... private area.

"Turn around. Don't cover yourself like that."

My arms moved, stiff, to my sides. I was so exposed. I couldn't stop crying. I couldn't stop crying.

I turned all the way around, slowly. She looked me up and down. Life had revealed possibilities beyond boys, beyond men. I was still trying to figure myself out, and now here I was, everything so twisted while I turned, naked, for this woman, just doing her job.

How can this be good for her?

How can I ever trust them again?

These aren't thoughts you have at the time – they're just how you feel when remembering. At the time, you're just in shock. Since then, I've wondered what else the Protector had seen; too many domestic violence cases, high-speed car accidents, mangled bodies, drunken attacks, sexual assault victims, misogyny, intimidation, with no clear path to any end goal or vision for how to really fix it all. And how many citizens had they terrorised as part of the job? The culture? What were they doing to my brother in training, to prepare him for this? To mould him for this?

"Put your clothes back on," said the Protector, turning back to the others. "She's clear."

"So's this one," they called back.

I scrambled to put my clothes back on, spluttering, wiping my eyes and nose. Tears heaved through me again. There was a hiccup of relief, but mostly I was choking back sheer shame. Sheer dehumanisation.

"We hope you'll come down and see the burn today."

"Yes sir," said Bacch, head down.

"God bless The Org," said the three Protectors, all in unison, all in uniform. The visors were back down. They were again indiscernible. My brother would soon be one of them. They marched out and disappeared downstairs.

"God bless Australia."

My legs wobbled and gave way. I hit the floor. Bacch appeared next to me. I felt him sit down, but I was looking away, staring at nothing.

There were no more plants. They'd taken all of them. Dirt was all through the carpet. The place seemed so bare. So hollow.

Stripped.

The eviction notice lay on the floor across from us. That was it. Our home was dead, if it ever really was one.

Bacch and I didn't touch each other. We didn't embrace. We just sat there.

How can they do that?

It's The Org. They've always done what they want. Why does this shock us, when it finally hits close to home?

But how can a human being do that to someone? How can that help anything?

I don't know ... I don't know ...

But we didn't say anything at all. I still couldn't look at Bacch. Eventually he stood up, checked his room, his stash spot probably, then went to the balcony. No more cactus reaching up to the sky.

"Cristina, look at this ..."

I didn't move at first, but he said it again, with a stranger tone. I stood slowly, using the coffee table for support. Out on the balcony, I looked in the direction of his attention. Giant columns of smoke arose from behind the buildings to the west of us, from Prince Alfred Park. The streets below were packed, heaving, a human river.

The burn.

The Org.

God bless.

"I'm going," said Bacch. His eyes were dark stones, heavy in his head. "I need to see this. I understand if you want to stay. I also understand why you'd hate me."

He looked at me. The stones melted away. It was just him.

"I'm sorry," he said.

He turned to go. I cleared my throat.

"Please. Don't go."

"Why?"

"Look at it. You can see from here that it's not safe. What if something happened to you?"

"I can't just do nothing."

"What can you do, though?"

We looked at each other.

He agreed to stay. We looked at footage, reports, articles, burns all around the country, gathering the masses. So much burned. We watched footage of Prince Alfred Park, a block away. We could smell the smoke, hear the crowds. The Protectors tied people to A-frame posts near the bonfires, in front of the people. They hung boards around their necks, inscribed with various crimes against The Org, against the King, against morality, against God, against country, against us, the citizens themselves. Confessing, denouncing, pleading, bleeding. Their arms were outspread, their hands bound, the mad firelight slapping their sweating skin. Another day on the news.

It was too much. It was all too much. The Org was not what it said it was. The world was not what it said it was. It was burning out there. The world was truly in chaos.

They even took the plants.

We had some cleaning up to do.

Bacch

Despair usually runs through me like a cheap curry, but this time it stuck around. I was still on a two-day comedown from Saturday night, and the strip searches, and everything. We sorted the mess at the apartment. Cristi went to her room. We never said anything further to each other. I understood. Ok.

I needed to fix my phone screen after throwing it at the train window. I poured a flask of rum. Wine wasn't enough today. Also punched a few cones. Drank some of the rum. Had a glass of water. Pulled a few more billies.

Monday.

Six days until eviction.

Let's go.

I hadn't been to an Apple store for years. The lighting alone was not compatible with my current settings. I kept my sunnies on. I was pretty high. Sleek tablets, smart watches, virtual reality headsets made of cardboard, gigantic white vibrators with screens & wi-fi; yeah I had not kept up with all of this. There were drip-fed trees inside the shop. Nice touch. Not apple trees, though. Lost opportunity there.

Countless employees stood around waiting for someone to need them. I approached the best-looking one.

"How'd the screen break?" he asked.

"A rose grew out of it."

"Yeah we've been getting a few of those lately."

In the end I just had to wait an hour for my data to get cloned onto a new phone – they'd deal with the broken one. Fine. I left & walked around. People hung out at shopping centres as a social activity. Not me. I drank & moved through Westfield listening to imported pop artists through the crackly mall loudspeaker, singing about escaping their lives.

No one else seemed to have any spring in their step either. It was an endless, heavy summer & we were all stuck in this air-conditioned shopping centre. Sunburnt girls walked around in bikinis for underwear, enjoying the racks of cloth. The bookshop had closed down since I was last here.

The burn?

A large screen three storeys high split the walkway through the shop levels, displaying the news. It was the Servant for Protectors, towering above us all, defending strip searches of teenagers & twelve-year-olds.

"I've got young children," said the giant bald head from the giant screen. "If I thought the Protectors felt they were at risk of doing something wrong, I'd want them strip searched. Having been Servant for Juvenile Justice, we have ten-year-olds involved in terrorism activity. I think you'd be pretty happy that they got found out."

I kept walking. I kept drinking.

More stores should follow Apple's lead & plant trees & bushes & megaflora throughout the place. I imagined vines climbing up the walls, like many hands moving up legs. Roots exploded across the varnished floors. Plants curled out from the sterile walls like tentacles tipped with budding flowers. The jungle reached the upper floors & shoppers were on their phones or looking at clothes & jewellery & a few were even looking at each other like they could see some soul there, but none could see what I saw. Even when the pythons & lions & boars started mowing people down, throwing humans through organic juice stalls & spraying blood & guts across the Starbucks counter, not that many people seemed to care. A zoo. The pop songs crackled overhead.

I walked past shop windows where mannequins modelled clothes. They'd hold a pose for some time, then change to another, then, another. Most were faceless, some bald, others headless. Some of the poses were sultry, enticing entry. With the animal killings & the sex in print & posture everywhere here, I wondered if children should be allowed in malls. I drank from the flask.

One mannequin was out of line. She wasn't pushing her figure out, wasn't looking at me from between her legs. She was sitting, with her chin on her knees, her arms wrapped around her legs, her toes against the glass. She had no face. I don't recall what she was modelling. Does it matter? I stopped & knelt in front of her.

She lifted her head to me. The one next to her moved into downward-facing dog. Even mannequins were getting into yoga now.

But this one, she put her hand up against the window. I put mine up against hers.

A crocodile crawled from the Lacoste shop nearby with a torn, bloody shirt hanging from its jaws. A moose was ploughing people with its antlers in the Abercrombie & Fitch store. An orgy of rabbits wearing black bowties spilled out of the newsagency.

We can't stay here. The mall is a fucked place.

I hit the flask & ran into the store & took the mannequin by the hand & ran out & the store clerk barely looked up from his screen to stop us. Our feet pounded the floor as we dodged the shoppers going to & fro. All faceless, too. She tripped over the roots & rocks a few times, but I guess mannequins aren't that accustomed to running. Security didn't care about the violence going on but, when they saw our escape attempt, two guards launched after us.

We weaved between mobile phone stalls & drinking fountains until the slower guard was attacked & shredded by a jaguar. The faster one followed us into the grocery store, but we lost him among the rows of canned meat & fled from it all.

I had to catch my breath after a while of running with her. I was pretty baked, after all, and a bit tipsy. She didn't need to breathe, but she seemed exhausted anyhow. After a moment, we stood looking at each other, moved closer – *kiss* – but she had no mouth, so we just hugged.

I wanted to know & understand her. So, we went to a bar. Everyone there was faceless, too, though, and I lost her in the crowd after I went for a piss.

A mannequin rescued from the madness. Artificial, yes, but real, too, no?

I ordered another few $28 beers, finished those, and went back to the mall to pick up my phone. They had done a good job of making it appear as if no jungle had ever been there, all spick & clean & well-lit & glassy, with pictures & screens of smouldering men & women in underwear having fun. I drank from the flask, unsure of anything.

I walked past the shop I had rescued the mannequin from. She was back. They'd caught her. And she was towing the line this time. They must have done something to her. She was really getting into the poses now. Tip of the runway. Well, maybe it wasn't really her. Maybe they'd just replaced her – they all look alike. Yeah, I like to think she escaped.

I need a job. Maybe as a mannequin?

The flask was almost empty. I held it over my open mouth, head cocked back, shaking the final drops onto my tongue & down my gullet, as I walked into the Apple store. And walked straight into someone.

"Watch it!" she said.

I stumbled. We looked at each other, startled.

"Hi, Wendy."

"Bacch, sorry." She stepped back, running her eyes up & down me. She wore a sleeveless blue summer dress. Her hair was tied up, letting her neck breathe.

"Me too. I'm a bit out of it today."

We both managed a good smile, revealing her little gap among big teeth. She pointed to the flask.

"Yeah ..." I said. "Look ..."

"Don't worry," she said. "This weekend was ... a lot."

She took a pharmacy container from her purse, removed a pill and swallowed. I saw The Org crest printed on the label.

"Do you two need anything?" said one of the staff. "We're about to close."

"Just picking up my phone," I said.

"Sir, you reek of alcohol."

"Yes, ok," said Wendy. "We'll get the phone & go."

We walked each other to the counter, got it sorted. All the while Wendy & I kept stealing clumsy looks at each other. There were breath mints next to the cashier's keys on the counter.

"Hey, can I please have a mint?" I asked.

"No."

"Oh, seriously?"

"They're my mints."

"C'mon, I've been drinking beers & rum all arvo."

"Maybe don't do that."

"Do you have any water?"

"Here's your phone."

Soon, Wendy & I were walking through the open bowels of the multistorey shopping complex, walking past shopkeepers pulling closed the shutter doors for the end of the day, some still open, shoppers still clinging on. We walked together. It felt nice, like we shared a secret, like we needed someone to be in on it with us.

"I rescued a mannequin here earlier," I said.

"Yes," she muttered. "Anything's possible these days."

Bright lighting on chrome railings & closed shutters & children yelling across the vast tiling, between pillars of screens of ads of sculpted humans in underwear & messages from The Org.

"I barely did any work today," she said.

"Me too."

"All I want to do is lie around at home."

"Me too."

"Should we go?" she said.

"Please."

I should have just gone home to Cristi. Only it was no longer our home, and Cristi wouldn't speak to me.

"Have you ever visited The Org dorms before?" asked Wendy.

"Oh. No ..."

We took the train together. The Org dorms are a bunch of colossal apartment buildings in Barangaroo. I felt like a mole. A spy. Infiltrating. Intruding. I was going to walk right on in there. A welcome guest.

"So, they don't allow guests," said Wendy, sitting next to me on the train.

"Oh."

"At least, boys aren't allowed unless they're family members. Vice versa, boys can't bring girl guests. The admin woman at our front desk though, she lets anyone sign in as a brother. One girl signs in her brother every weekend, and every weekend he looks like a different person."

"Freaky."

"It'll be fine."

"What are your thoughts on Org policy," I said, "when you're out at raves with your cousin? When you see what the Protectors do?"

"Look," she said. "I don't follow every rule of the Bible. I don't follow every rule my parents set down. Not every rule of The Org I agree with. Who can follow all these rules? We go through shit; we all go through shit. Sometimes we need to deal with things in ways they don't like. But we need to improve things, however we can."

We talked about our respective getaways from the Protectors on Saturday night. They had pre-organised hiding spots, she said. They waited it out, then had kick-ons back at Giao's. No news of how the speakers ended up. Wendy & I soon trickled off into cooked, comfortable silence. We reached Wynyard Station, emerged from the underground & walked towards The Org precinct. The sun was close to disappearing. Trees hooked up to drips lined the walkways. The rum was really working on me.

"That building there," Wendy pointed out. "Home sweet home."

Another skyscraper of apartments, all steel & concrete, reached up to the clouds. The ground floor had walls of glass revealing the red, white & blue foyer interior. Lots of couches & coffee tables. Wendy scanned her Org ID to let us in. My phone buzzed as I walked through the front doors. I checked it. My service was gone. I had to sign up to The Org's network, or have no connection. I didn't sign up.

"How you doin, Maggie?" Wendy said to the receptionist.

"I'm ok," said Maggie, sitting behind the dark blue front counter. The shelves behind her were all bright red. The walls were glaringly white. The carpet was black. Maggie looked up. "Hi Wendy. Oh. Hello."

"Lovely to meet you," I said. "How good is The Org, ay. Who designed this interior?"

"Step-brother?" Maggie asked, smiling.

We signed in.

"How crazy is it," said Maggie, "that the sun will explode one day … You think that's Armageddon?"

"I don't know," said Wendy as she finished with the form. "Would that interpretation help you in your life?"

"I don't know. Hey, nice seeing you."

We went up in the elevator. Lots of mirrors. We kept making eye contact through bent reflections & laughing a little. Out of the elevator. Long white walls, ceiling, black floors, red & blue & white furnishings. A giant miscoloured hotel honeycomb. We passed communal living spaces, a kitchen, heaps more dorm doors, dining areas – I thought I recognised someone in there but couldn't place him – until we reached Wendy's room.

Inside, I looked around, lit only by the city's twilight glow through her window. It was a tiny space, single bed, spartan & minimal. White. Red. Blue. The walls seemed tilted. Space between objects seemed to fluctuate.

Should we be doing this? Am I facilitating something destructive for this woman? Or is she dragging me down? I just want beauty & passion.

157

Wendy & I found each other. Is she that beauty, that passion? Do I even have the capacity to recognise it? Do I recognise myself?

Each undressed the other, lips & limbs pressed up like we were swimming in each other. After a while she jumped on the red quilt of the bed, a cheeky grin exposing the gap in her front teeth. I leant down to grab a condom from my wallet among the jeans.

"Oh, don't worry," said Wendy. She propped herself up by her elbows, her legs laid out like a runway to me, sliding atop the sheets, her lil tits moving atop her ribs with her breath. "We don't use contraception."

"What?"

"It's against The Org, I mean, the church. You know that. The seed is sacred."

"Wait, what?"

"Just pull out at the end."

"Isn't that still wasting … the seed? And didn't you say you don't follow all the rules?"

"Only the unreasonable ones." She threw a pillow at me. "You're a free spirit, a good time guy, right?"

"I used to think so."

"Well …" she said, stretching her legs out even further. "Isn't it boring, thinking sex is this open, natural thing you can do whenever, with whoever? There's nothing naughty in that. No thrill. No sin. You're just a wild animal fucking, with no sense of divinity."

I stood there naked. She lay there naked.

"It doesn't sound so bad," I said.

"I guess. Sex is sex, divine or otherwise."

"What if sex itself is the most divine thing?" I said, moving toward her, propping my knees up on the bed. "The vehicle of conception, of life? Haven't you ever wished for a religion where sex & motherhood are worshipped? It'd at least be a more pleasant belief system."

"We'll just have to find out," she whispered between licks & bites.

"Not the motherhood part."

158

"Just pull out."

"C'mon ... no. We gotta use –"

"No. Just do it."

"The holy thing to do?"

"Yes."

"No."

"Please ..."

"Jesus ..."

"Baptise me in your come."

"Amen ..."

Cristi

Vines and creeper leaves had taken over most of the alleyway walls leading to The Snakepit. It was night time, but no lights were on, no suspended neon to light up the door, somewhere down there. It was like stepping out of reality, off the streets of Darlinghurst, through a gap in the concrete, a shred, the entrance to a monolithic labyrinth, walls stretching up into the clouds. I couldn't see the street at the other end through the darkness. Sirens screamed nearby.

Sirens are everywhere in the city. I thought I'd already known this, hearing them, all the time, but now I felt them.

I walked into the alleyway.

It was Wednesday, four days until eviction. Bacch hadn't slept at home since the raid. The apartment was just so empty. Empty. No life. It had been a mindless week at work so far. I couldn't stay in another night. Alone. Lonely. They're two different things. You can be happy, alone. You can love yourself, alone. You should. You deserve to. But loneliness has an appetite. Loneliness can swallow.

I wanted to dance. I wore a cheap but elegant open-backed dress. Perhaps Zira would be there tonight. Perhaps Mikael. Perhaps Bacch. Perhaps someone. Anyone. I was ready for anything. Anything except this darkness.

My skin began to tremble as I ventured further down the alley. The neon chandelier did not flicker on. I took out my phone to illuminate my steps. I soon found the metal door that led to The Snakepit. No chandelier. There was a sign bolted to the door, authority seals and fine print and:

The labyrinth was a dead end.

I touched the cross that rested against my sternum. The phone light revealed nature's leafy fingers spreading out across the vast parted sea of concrete and brick. I thought of the snake that had confronted the Protector. The tempting serpent, shining with rainbow reflections. Where was it now? Was it ok?

The devil could be anyone. Anything.

Even nature? Even me?

Loneliness has an appetite.

Darkness can swallow.

I turned off the light. I walked off into the night.

Bacch

Wendy buzzed me in downstairs. It was Wednesday & I hadn't yet been caught out. Four days until eviction.

Things had worked fine with Maggie, so far. But someone new was at reception, a middle-aged woman with hawkish features & drooping makeup. No Maggie.

"Hello," the new receptionist said. "Are you signing in?"

"Ah ... yes. I am. Where's Maggie today?"

"She's gone."

"Gone?"

"Yes."

"Like ... fired?"

She tapped her red pen on the blue desk. "I'm not aware of the details."

"Right. Well, I'm the guest of –"

"You can just show me your ID to begin and we'll get you sorted," she said.

"Oh. I didn't need ID before?"

"I know. We were tipped off about flaws in security here. The Org thanks those who help national security."

"Is that why the last receptionist is ... gone?"

"I'm not aware of the details."

"Hang on, I just need to make a quick call to the resident ..." But when I checked my phone, I still had no signal here, only The Org's network.

"Is everything ok?" she asked.

"I don't have my ID."

"Why not?"

"I ... I don't have one."

"But you *must* have identification."

"No, I mean I ... don't have an identity.

"Um ..."

"Please, it's ok," I said, slowly walking toward the elevators. "I'm nobody."

"But you must be *somebody* ..."

"Please," I whispered. Right in her eyes. "Really. I'm ... no one ..."

I must have said it with enough conviction. I made it to the elevator, pressed the button, door opened. I looked back as the doors slid shut. She was standing behind the blue desk, reaching for something, shaking her head, saying something about security flaws.

The elevator sent me flying up into the sky, running up through the building. There was every chance I did not get away with that breach. I had to find Wendy. Tucked away in this mirrored metal box, I wondered about the earth below, falling further away from me.

I walked past the communal areas towards Wendy's dorm. I saw through the vast glass windows a row of young people working at their laptops, the dark blue desks, the red chairs, the white walls, the black carpet. One guy was looking at me, the one I thought I recognised here before. Slick hair. Cold, steely eyes. Looking at me.

The Org thanks those who help national security.

The communal areas disappeared from view as the glass became wall again. I felt like doubling back, but didn't want to expose myself any more than I may have already. That's the thing with The Org. The paranoia just gradually increases, over months & years. You barely realise you're getting more & more wound up, questioning everything, wondering what they know, how they know it, who you can trust, who they're playing off against who, what insanity the MO newspapers will print next, what incentives lie behind the many closed doors.

Wendy's door opened. She pulled me in. Shut it. We were hidden. I hoped.

All the while, I couldn't stop thinking about Cristi. I'd abandoned her, in an apartment that now felt haunted. All of Sydney felt haunted. Were we always doomed? Perhaps not her. I could've been hunting down apartments, terraces, houses for us to move to, to keep us together. I couldn't face reality, couldn't be honest with her or myself. Strangling a heart to protect it – it didn't make sense, but I did it. All I wanted to do was to love Cristi. And here I was, with someone else.

There is a fine line between a hopeless romantic and a fuckboy; I was not proud to have crossed it.

We'd been fooling around in our underwear for a while when Wendy emerged from her closet with handcuffs.

"Ok," she said, kneeling on the dark blue bed. "I'm a Protector. You're ... I dunno, let's say you're a journalist. You speak out against The Org."

"Wendy," I said. "What?

"Role-playing. I'm going to do a house raid & handcuff you to the bed. You filthy dissenting terrorist."

I thought of the Protectors interrogating me in my home, strip searching Cristi in our home.

Pull back your foreskin. Now turn around. Why are you crying? If you've got nothing to hide, why don't you just cooperate?

"Look," I said, sitting next to her. "I'd usually be into this."

"It's hot, right?" she said with a grin.

"But, Wendy ... you know they replaced Maggie? Apparently, someone's been reporting security breaches."

"Oh, dang. How did you get in?"

"Um ... I kinda winged it. I can't do it again though."

"The Org shuffles staff around all the time. I'm sure you're fine today, we'll figure it out for next time." She leaned in & whispered in my ear. Her hot wet breath melted my lobe & tickled my body. "But now, it's time to get arrested ..."

I was genuinely afraid. Was Wendy in on it? Was this it for me? The adrenaline raced. My blood pumped through me. And I was getting hard. Of all the ways I could have ever been taken in by The Org, by the Protectors, this would at least be the best I could hope for.

We started hooking up on the bed, but she pushed me off.

"Not yet," she said. In the little studio dorm, she'd have to go out into the hallway to actually role-play entering. Instead, she grabbed a leather coat, went into the tiny ensuite bathroom that she shared with her neighbour & closed the door.

"Pretend like you're just living your life at home," she called out. "Do whatever atheists do when they're bored."

She didn't have liquor or a chop bowl anywhere. Not that I needed any more at that stage. The only book she had was The Org's white Bible on her desk. There were no pot plants. There was no Cristi.

I was about to say to Wendy, *Let's call it quits*, then go home, see Cristi, declare my unworthy love, my confused passions, fall at her feet & beg forgiveness, look up new places to live, new jobs to apply for …

But there were several ferocious knocks at the door. They didn't seem like Wendy's. The fists were too big, too wild. The fear was still running through me.

It's hot, right?

"Who is it?" I called out.

"Open up!"

It was Wendy, of course. I was going mad.

I stood up & approached the bathroom door. As I got near, she flung it open & ran at me, pushing me over to the bed.

"Face down with your hands behind your back."

"What if I resist?"

She smiled. "I'll fuck you up."

Wendy stood there, this sexy little Org demon, bra & undies & nothing else but skin & body beneath that huge black jacket. My own underpants were heaving, swelling, and I couldn't help but notice the white book of The Org, heaving, swelling, growing in size atop Wendy's desk, but Wendy turned me around & I let her. She pushed me to the bed, and I let her. I didn't call it quits. I didn't resist. Everything The Org has done, we let it. Everything that happened with the house, with Cristi, I let it.

No one came for me in the night. No one dragged me out.

We were just kids.

I stayed over, but silently resolved to slow this down, sort my life out, just do the right thing. And avoid the authorities.

In the morning, we went at it again. As we were in the final throes, I saw the white Org book on the desk. It looked at least three times bigger than last night.

I hadn't yet joined Wendy for any of their communal breakfasts, but today I was hungry & free meals are hard to come by. It was a buffet-style breakfast, with different stations all laid out on dark blue tables & shining red crockery, and a cafeteria area for eggs & omelettes. Why were the lights always too bright? White walls, black linoleum. Long rows of blue tables & red chairs. I felt like I was in a Play School prison eatery. I promised myself I'd get groceries for Cristi & me on the way home. Some people, dressed & ready for the working world, greeted Wendy & me.

"And you must be her ..."

"Step-brother," said Wendy.

"Of course."

And then there was that same slick guy. He was collecting food when Wendy saw him, spooning mushy scrambled eggs onto his plate.

Plop.

"Oh, hi Patrick! I don't think you've met Bacch yet."

"Hi."

"Hi."

We sorted our plates & all sat together. Wendy & Patrick each removed a prescription container, popped something in their mouths and swallowed.

"Bacch," said Patrick. "Would you like to say grace?"

"Nah. You're probably better at it than me."

"C'mon, Bacch," said Wendy, teasing. "Are you not ... devout?"

"Alright, alright ..." I bowed my head to face a plate of steaming mush, put my hands together and closed my eyes. My chest tightened.

"Let's ... let's give thanks for the food we are about to eat. Be grateful for whatever we have. Cultivate compassion with all beings. Life is a house party that the Protectors could bust at any moment, so crank the music to its loudest, add more mescaline to the punch so we truly taste it, and dance dance fuckin dance knowing we all die while few truly live."

Silence.

"Amen," I added.

"Amen," repeated Wendy.

Patrick sniggered, spooning food.

"They're announcing the official method of execution today," he said. "Finally. They're scheduled to kill em tomorrow."

His voice triggered my memory.

"I know why you look so familiar!" I said with wide eyes. "You were the app date! Cicely, at that joint in the harbour."

"Yeah," he said. "I recognised you too."

"You didn't say anything?"

Patrick shrugged, kept eating.

"How did the date go?" I asked.

"We had sex in the restaurant bathroom."

"Patrick!" said Wendy.

"The accessible bathroom," he said, grinning over his eggs.

"The railing next to the sink?" I said, laughing.

"Um, yeah ..."

I cackled. People looked over at us. Wendy & Patrick looked confused. I was losing my mind, but fuck it. The whole world was losing its mind.

"Wendy," he continued, over my chortles. "You know that other chick from The Org? The weird one? Of all people, I took her to one of the last underground bars. What a waste. Very argumentative. Didn't listen to a word I said, and I said a lot of them. Then she vomited on me. How uncouth."

"Patrick!" said Wendy, with a fierce voice, like she was role-playing again.

Patrick stared at me, before addressing Wendy. "She's just ... weird. One of those righteous believers. I wonder if she'll last at The Org ..."

"Who's this?" I asked.

"You wouldn't know her," said Patrick.

"Why'd she vomit on you?" I asked.

"Why so many questions?"

"I'm a friendly guy."

"She ordered absinthe. Couldn't handle it."

"Absinthe," I said. "My kinda girl."

"I need to go to the bathroom," said Wendy, standing up. "Then we'll leave."

She disappeared. Patrick kept chewing for a while. The accumulated hangover was slamming me. Eventually he took one unholy gulp & wiped his mouth to speak.

"I wouldn't come back here if I were you."

"Yeah? Why is that, brudda?"

He smirked. "Who do you think you are? You think the rules don't apply to you?"

"The rules keep changing," I said, staring him down through the headache. "Your Servants & your Protectors. Don't think they won't keep you in line when *you* get too big for your boots. I'm safer than you, in the shadows."

He smiled. "I wouldn't be so sure, Bacch."

"Ok fellas," said Wendy, approaching us. "We gotta go."

"I might see you later," said Patrick. "I'm going to the prayer room."

"To ... pray?" I smiled.

His eyes were cold. "Nice seeing you again, Bacch."

Fuck that guy. Wendy & I walked out of that monstrosity of a dining hall & toward the elevators. There were a lot of people leaving for work, so we had to squeeze in. I manoeuvred to stay in the middle of the group as we walked through the downstairs lobby, just in case there was security. There was security; only one guard near the exit doors. The receptionist was attending to someone. *Did they see me?* We walked out. We walked out just fine. Fuck your national security. I needed a smoke.

The residential skyscraper was on the same block as The Org. The pavements were a light grey, huge minimalist slabs. The black tar of the road looked like smooth icing atop a cake. Every few slabs of paving, there was a round plot with huge leafy trees hooked up to IV lines, pulsating slowly, strangely. It was a sunny day. Everyone was moving towards The Org, a procession. I went to say goodbye to Wendy, to continue to the train station.

That's when I saw Cristi, in her work outfit. Walking toward The Org. She stopped at one of the IV tree plots, bent down, studying the nutrient rig. Cristi, walking to work ...

I ... I work at The Org ... I take care of him.

"Hey, Cristina!" called out Wendy.

Holy shit.

Cristi

This city chews you up and spits you back out with a few extra coats of salivary experience. You leave home thinking you know something. I had no idea of the world out here. I had no idea of myself in here.

I woke up every morning rolling around as if to find some semblance of human touch in the sheets. But there was none. Bacch could be in the next room, doing the same perhaps, though never waking until after me. That's if he's even home.

Where does he go?

I was alone again. I thought God would be there with me. I wanted to feel that again. But no.

I wanted to buy new plants. *Is that even still allowed?* But no.

I couldn't bring myself to leave the apartment. But I couldn't stand being in the apartment. I spent more and more time in my bed. *Why even get up?* The world had had enough of me, and I'd had enough of it.

But it was a work day, so I had to get up. Every instinct in my body told me to stay in that bed, stay safe. I couldn't trust the world any more. But I still lived in it. I was still a part of this world. It was a sunny day. *Ugh.*

I got out of bed. Sorted myself. Disregarded breakfast again. The front door was now overrun by moss. Perhaps it was time for The Org dorms, if there were any left. I took the train to Wynyard. The crowds were intense, sweating, many with breathing masks on. I got out and walked with everyone to The Org.

The IV trees all waved, slowly, strangely.

At the entrance to The Org, I stopped. I stood on the lawn to let everyone else through. I looked at one of the trees. The beautiful bark.

The veins of sap. The rippling, almost luminescent leaves. I bent down to see the nutrient bag again, to see my reflection. Warped. I saw someone else's reflection. It was Wendy.

"Hey, Cristina!"

And it was ...

Surely not. I turned around on faith that I'd misidentified the distorted face in the reflection. But it was him. Bacch and Wendy. *What kind of sick shit is this?* They stepped onto the lawn. I felt my throat constrict, tried to swallow.

"You hate The Org," I said to Bacch. "Why are you here?"

"Me?" he whispered, eyes startled, head swivelling for nearby reconnaissance. "*I love The Org!*"

"He's with me," smiled Wendy.

"*Why?*"

"Why do you work at The Org," asked Bacch, "when you ... don't work at The Org?"

"Would you really have let me live with you?"

Bacch looked straight at me. "I've wanted you with me since the day you first ... inspected."

"Don't worry," I continued, but my voice faltered. "You won't have to live with me anymore."

I stopped and shook my head. It felt like my insides were eating my insides, my stomach eating my stomach, my heart eating my heart. I turned and joined the people entering the huge front doors of The Org. I don't know what Bacch did from there. I didn't care.

Wendy caught up to me. We didn't speak. Up the elevator together. She stepped out at her floor.

"Just let me know ... if you ever want to talk," she said. Those beautiful eyes. No wonder Bacch wanted her. I wanted her. I wanted him. The elevator doors closed. Wendy disappeared.

"Gather round, my busy bees!" called Mrs Ogglesworth for our morning staff meeting. "We have some *very* exciting news."

My colleagues couldn't contain their excitement. Many sweated or fidgeted or whispered to themselves unintelligibly. Mrs Ogglesworth turned the TV on. The King's address. Live on national television and all socials.

"My dear, sweet children," he began, his face huge and bloated across the screen.

How do these men attain power?

He announced that Protectors had charged the Casino Three with terrorism, though he couldn't quite pronounce their names properly. He paused before announcing the method of capital punishment for tomorrow.

"The snake pit!" he yelled through the screen.

The Org had already demolished Allianz Stadium in Moore Park. In its place stood a massive amphitheatre, a stadium around a footy field that could open up into a pit. Rushed and over budget. The snakes delivering the punishment would be a diverse mix of Australia's deadliest species, starved prior. All the news and TV channels would have their eyes on execution night, your Friday night entertainment. The sponsors were locked in. There would be sugarless fairy floss for the kids.

At the end of the broadcast, the King just laughed for several minutes, jabbering nonsense, crying as he chomped on a raw onion. Everyone's eyes were glued to the screen.

"Ok, my busy bees," said Mrs Ogglesworth when the coverage returned to a feature about how much of a family man the King is. "You heard our leader! The method is ... snake pit! How *exciting!*"

Everyone cheered, singing songs, skipping in circles, while taxes paid our salaries. I sat at my desk, wondering how it got to this. I had been so happy to work for The Org. I believed in government, in people, in Protectors, in a good God. Where was everything I so valued? It all looked so different in real life. All the things you believe in as a child, flipped upside down. Authorities with multiple tongues and black gunk oozing from pointed ears, fake news since the womb, baby zebras spat straight onto their legs and shoved through hoops and shot with hormones ...

I wasn't feeling well ...

Mrs Ogglesworth approached me at my desk. A few others in the office had foregone the festivities and were at their desks, too. Some at The Org were here to work, in spite of the carry-on. Mrs Ogglesworth leaned over to me.

"Is something wrong, Cristina?"

I kept staring at nothing.

He's with me.

"You know you can tell Mrs Ogglesworth anything, don't you Cristina?"

"Don't refer to yourself in third person."

"What's gotten into you today, young lady?"

I've wanted you with me since ...

Begin the strip searches.

I stood up to face her. "Why do you get so excited about this policy?"

"Why wouldn't I be excited? Everyone else is! It's a step forward towards a safer, peaceful future. The Org is even giving us all free entry to the show!"

"No."

Colleagues began to take notice, but I didn't care.

"It's a step backward," I continued. "The Org is supposed to lead by example. What example are our leaders setting for us? For the world? What does Australia stand for anymore? What did we ever stand for?"

"It's an example of deterrence," said Mrs Ogglesworth. "Just as detaining refugees in terrible conditions for years and years, with no rights, is a deterrent to boat arrivals. And guess what? Our leaders stopped the boats. The King even keeps a little laser-cut metal statue of a migrant boat in his office, engraved with 'I Stopped These'. So, deterrents work. Just like the prospect of jail deters would-be criminals.

Everyone is a would-be criminal. Especially refugees. We're all one crime away from being criminals. Deterrence is necessary."

"I think you've deterred me." I sat down, lightheaded.

"What is that supposed to mean?"

"Can't you just transfer me to another sector?"

"Isn't this where you want to be, Cristina?"

"I don't know where I want to be. I don't know what I want to do."

"Perhaps you should stop thinking about what you *want*, and start working."

The snake pit churned inside me. "I quit."

Mrs Ogglesworth's face melted with devastation. *"WHY?"*

"Yeah. I quit."

I walked past Mrs Ogglesworth to grab my bag. The office was silent but for Media Ochre News constantly muttering in the background.

No one knew what to do. Some staff consoled other staff. Mrs Ogglesworth stood disconsolate. Colleagues filmed on their phones.

I walked out of there and no one came after me.

Well, I had to wait awkwardly at the elevator doors, at the end of the wide foyer hall, until they opened up. But I didn't look back, not until I turned around to see the office being squished into nothing by the automatic doors, like metal curtains across a scene of tragic theatre.

I found myself surrounded by tall men in suits in an elevator that wasn't moving.

Are we stuck? Are the Protectors coming for me? Can you just quit and walk out like that and not expect repercussions? Are they controlling the building? How much power do they truly have?

But no, it began to move down. I was too jittery. No one spoke.

The first stop was Level 73, the skybridge park. All of the men walked out. I followed, unthinking, and walked off into the gardens by myself. Some Protectors ambled along with the workers, but they either hadn't seen me or weren't looking for me. I realised I'd barely been breathing. I sucked in as much oxygen as possible. The air was better up here than down in the streets. I sat below a giant palm tree, IV drip plugged into a metal box next to me. My warped reflection looked out from the nutrient bag. I couldn't stand the sight. I grabbed it. I pulled it from the box. *Plop.* Slime dripped from the disconnect.

The bark began to morph and shrivel into something like parchment. I stood and backed away. The tree withered into a skeletal figure, like the emaciated arm, wrist and fingers of a dead woman. The sap veins discoloured as their flow slowed. Leaves dropped, black and brown, to the manicured lawn in soft dances. Everyone stopped to look. People held sandwiches at their mouths, caught in rapture by the spectacle of botched botany.

I ran back across the skybridge as people gathered at the tree, some even kneeling at the base as if it were a sacrificial sign of divinity. Perhaps it was. I no longer understood the signs and stories. I just had to get out. I ran beneath the luscious Chinese blossoms until I was back in the elevator, descending from that artificial garden of skyline paradise, back to earth. I ran out of the building downstairs, ran between the other trees still hooked up, veins pumping, leaves shining.

I remembered my abandoned lunch container in the tearoom fridge. The Org had my chickpea salad now.

I lost myself in the streets of Sydney, hoping Bacch might find me.

Bacch

I couldn't find my keys. Fuckin hopeless. I was scuttling outside the apartment when Kafi called with some developments.

"Broooo," he said. "They've imprisoned Ria under the wrong name."

"What?"

"The Org's identity recognition software said she was someone else. She's locked up as someone else. We just visited her with the lawyer ..."

He described the conversation between the lawyer & The Org court administrator.

"Why can't you just let her go & apologise?" said the lawyer.

"Even if we did make a mistake, which we didn't, and I'm not admitting that, but if we *did*, we'd never admit it."

"Why?"

"We would look silly."

"Don't you see, we'd respect you for taking responsibility and making amends? You could fix the fault in the system?"

"Nah, yeah, nah. Yeah, nah."

The law is confusing, but Kafi said the lawyer was working on it.

"There were heaps of reporters out front, too," he continued. "They've moved the Casino Three to the same prison before the, uh, the snake pit day. Will you be protesting?"

"Maybe. You?"

"We have to run the bakery."

"Kafi," I said, hesitating. "I don't know if I can stay in the city. I won't have my place much longer."

"Just live in a van or something, bro. I'd love to live like that. That freedom ..."

"I've been considering it. I have money left over from the leftovers."

"Hey, how's this snake pit shit, ay. Civilisation is fucking barbaric. Isn't Western society supposed to be civilised, wasn't that the whole purpose of the colonists? In Jesus's name?"

"Look, who knows."

"Brooo, I think I want to join The Org. I want to help my country, help Ria, so I can't just talk about it. I have to get involved."

"That's ... great, Kafi."

"The Org, the Protectors, the media, they demonise me. I can't just demonise them back. It's hypocritical, bro. There is some good shit going on. It's like if you wrote an article or some bullshit novel about how evil & ineffective The Org & the Protectors are, like from just one side in a stereotype."

"Yes, well ..."

"Why don't you join The Org, Bacch? Do you want change? Do you ever protest?"

"Well, sometimes I protest on my socials."

"Oh. Well, yeah. They reckon it'll be compulsory soon, to join the Program, if you've been unemployed for a certain period of time. The Org hates welfare, you know."

"Surely not. Like forced labour?"

All my income for a while had been cash, off the books. *Would I have to join?*

"I mean, they pay you. After they take the tax. Don't worry, you'd be in the offices, not the fields or the factories. Maybe the army. Maybe even a teacher, ha!"

"Yeah speaking of, how are you doing at school? Your environmental essay go well?"

"Ah, this connection, I can't hear you very well brooo. Talk soon?"

"Talk soon, brooo."

As I ended the call, I noticed a notification on my phone screen. The UN condemned Australia's use of a snake pit as an execution method, but The Org had ignored them. As always. Just went on ahead with it.

The Org. Join us.

Found my keys. The door opened up. I closed it & collapsed on the couch, tired. Sleeping on a single bed with someone else has never been my forte. I never know whether I should move, how loud I am, if I should put my arm over or under or just crumple one beneath me as I lie sideways.

I must have dozed because suddenly I heard the latch turn. The hinges creaked.

Cristi stepped back into my world. We looked at each other for the first time since that morning's encounter with her & Wendy. She was home early. Her hair was a mess. Her eyes were bleared & puffy. Mine were too. I rubbed them & sat up. She closed the door but just stood there, looking at me, breathing deeply through her nose. She was beautiful. We said nothing. She put her bag on the kitchen counter before sitting on the couch, at the other end, away from me. We sat there, just looking at the bare wall in front of us, previously shrouded by ferns & fronds & frangipani flowers. Even the small leaves peeking through cracks seemed to have retreated, as if the world was no longer palatable for them. Only the cracks were growing, reaching further & further. The apartment was full of longing, yearning, hunger, craving, yet so empty.

"I'm sorry." We both said it at the same time, catching eyes, then looked back at the wall.

"I don't want to lie to you," I added.

"Me too," she said.

"You're still the lesser of the two evils here."

"Is that supposed to make me feel better?"

"I guess," I muttered.

"I quit The Org today," she said, still staring at the wall.

"Wow … Not for me, I hope?"

She laughed & shook her head. "Not everything is about you, Bacch. The Org is using a snake pit to administer the death penalty. A *snake pit* ... The executions are tomorrow. They said they're removing red tape, but it's just to block any time for people to object before going ahead." She heaved a sigh. "We were taught that the Servants were there to serve the people. We were taught that the Protectors were there to protect the people. We were taught that Media Ochre reports the truth. We were taught that we own The Org, that we fund it, that we decide how the country is managed. But the Servants serve themselves. The Protectors protect themselves. Media Ochre says what The Org wants. Even the King says what The Org wants. The Org owns us. The Org owns us."

I just nodded.

After a while, she turned to address me. "Why Wendy, of all people?"

"I didn't know you two knew each other," I said. "I didn't even know you worked there, y'know, let alone with her."

"Not that," she said. "What was it about her? How did you even meet?"

"Wendy goes to raves with her cousin."

"WHAT?"

"Yeah. Sexy nun outfits & everything."

Cristi's eyes went back to the wall.

"You can't divide your heart," she said eventually.

"Love is a renewable resource."

Her eyes stayed on the wall.

"Look," I continued. "She could dance. She was cute. She kept popping up. I'll take my validation where I can get it."

"You've said before, only you can validate you. Love yourself."

"Like Jesus loves you?"

She shot me a dirty look. "Oh, go ask your *bong* on a date then!"

"Cannabis has done more for me than Jesus ever did."

179

"My faith has done more for me than *you* ever did." She stood & grabbed her work bag from the kitchen on the way to her room. The door slammed shut.

If cupid is a cunt, I'm at least a prick.

I went to my room, opened the secret stash panel, and grabbed my bong.

Cristi

My window was open, but I was sweating. Confusions occupied my mind. My hands massaged the back of my neck, rubbed my thighs. I needed a release.

I could confess everything. I could call my parents. But what would they say? What would they think? They'd just tell me to go back in there and keep my job, apologise, keep on doing what was expected of me.

Don't you love your country?

Respect The Org, honey. Please.

But is a country the same thing as a government? If a government is doing wrong by its people, isn't it more patriotic to condemn the government than to support it?

Praise The Org, sweetie.

My phone buzzed next to me. It was my mother.

"Hello?" I answered.

"Cristina!" Mum sounded breathless, like she'd get when trying to explain scripture at the dinner table. "Don't panic! Don't panic. We're ok, we're ok. For now."

"Mum? What's going on?"

"It's ok, it's ok. I just want to let you know that we've cleared the gutters round the house, hosed them down, and packed all the valuables into the car. It's ok, it's ok."

"What's happening up there?"

"There's a fire coming. The road into town, it's blocked off. It's … ah … it's been a big day, honey… but I wanted to ask. Have to ask. Your room, do you want me to save anything? I can put some more stuff in the car in case we have to evacuate. Not everything, but yeah, just let me know. There's only Old Soldier's Road to get out on and that's all dirt track and bush, so we'd probably have to drive to the beach, to evacuate. God help us. Can you think of anything to save? Sorry it's so sudden but, you know, we just have to prepare for the worst, and you gotta because if you're not, you're sitting here stressing and imagining the house in … in flames …"

Mum started crying. She handed the phone to Dad.

"Hi, Cristina."

"Hi, Dad."

"The smoke in the sky … it's biblical. We're very tense."

"Are you … praying?"

"Of course."

"Look, Dad, I don't need anything. Just look after yourselves."

"Surely you'd like something saved?"

"Nothing."

"Oh."

"I have what I need with me. The rest can burn."

"Well … I'm sure your mother will still save half your room, all the same."

I laughed. It hurt to laugh, like I wasn't used to it.

"Thanks, Dad. Are you ok?"

"Just … tense. The Rural Fire Service and community group chats have been amazing resources so far. We'll update you later. You must be at work at this hour. How has The Org been? We haven't spoken for a while."

"It's been … engaging. Very fierce. I'm … learning a lot."

"That's wonderful. Have you met any suitable men?"

"Definitely not."

"Well, yes, like I said, keep you updated later, but don't worry. God will protect us. And hey, honey?"

"Yes, Dad?"

"We're so proud of you, for the work you're doing. Praise The Org. God bless."

"I love you, Dad."

"I love you too, darling." Mum called out the same, her voice a croak.

I hung up and wiped the sweat from my forehead.

Life just keeps coming at you.

No one is coming to help you.

I didn't have Bacch to rely on, not anymore, if ever. Prayers never really worked. They only resulted in a real outcome if I prayed to ponder something, to process it in a more focused presence of the Lord. Otherwise, God didn't seem to take requests.

If I had created the world, it would look very different. But I hadn't.

I am a creation of God ... of the universe.

I thought of Zira. Her business card. I fluttered around the room, trying to remember where I'd stashed it after the raid. *Hello.* I dialled the number.

No ring. Dead line. I couldn't even leave a message.

I tried again. Dead line.

Nothing felt right.

I searched for news on the bushfires, but there was nothing yet other than the RFS website. It had a national map showing fires and their recent status; red and yellow fire symbols, red being the worst, surrounded the south end of my hometown, last updated 1hr 22mins ago. There wasn't much more yet.

I looked up protests for the execution, how to join, reviewed the details. Every post advised against going alone.

Nothing felt right.

Bacch

My window was open, but I was sweating. Confusions occupied my mind. My hands massaged the back of my neck, knuckles in my forehead. I needed a release.

My phone buzzed nearby. I lay on my bed, face down, eyes hidden from the daylight peeking from behind the shuttered curtain. I still hadn't slept properly. I grabbed the phone. It was Hari.

"Hey bro. Keen for a house party tonight? Well, it's actually an apartment. A studio apartment. Real intimate. I've got bags. Should be alright. I have an app date beforehand, might bring her along too."

"Are we ever gonna make something of ourselves?" I asked. "Or are we just gonna be fucked cunts?"

"Bro, why do you have to demonise having a good time? All the time? Just ... have a good time. Life is short & mostly shit. Don't make the other parts shit too."

"I can't come. I'm getting kicked out of my place."

"Oh ... sorry to hear. You got somewhere to go? The lease inspections have been madness everywhere."

"I was thinking ... The Org might be my best option, just while I get my shit together."

"I don't believe it."

"What choice is there?"

"I'd offer here, but ..." Hari's voice dropped to a whisper. "Even I've considered joining The Org to get out of this place. Shit's just ... falling apart & the building authorities don't do anything to fix anything. And of course the rent went up."

"I know the feeling."

"So, you gotta say goodbye to the girl?"

"I'd rather not."

"Shit, man. Well, look. Are you going to the executions?"

"I dunno. Tickets are sold out. I considered protesting."

"I have something you might be interested in. I have a double pass. Servant seating."

"How? Is it ... that client?"

"A gift. Earned it, she says. Why not, ay?"

"She? I thought your client was ..."

"Look, Bacch, baby. She's a Servant. She sets me up with other Servants. I spy. She gets something on them, something compromising. Bro, The Org is a repressed place."

"Hari, none of what you just told me sounds appealing & I don't want any part of it."

That's what I wanted to say. That's what I begged my lips & mouth & tongue to say. But the words slipped by me. I was mute. This was a wild, historic opportunity.

"You have a suit, yeah? See if you can book in a haircut beforehand. You might make some good contacts, if you do sign up with The Org. Ah! We need to INDULGE."

"Why not, ay."

"WHY NOT AY!"

"How's your mum?"

"Yeah, worse, but she doesn't seem to wanna die, ay. She just charges through the bullshit. Let the river flow, embrace it. Nature finds a way, she says. That's some wisdom shit."

He sent me the details for attending the execution, chatted through it, hung up. I rolled over & wished for sleep. Buried my face in the mattress. At long last I drifted through dreamy fragments of Hari & Bianca seducing Cristi in a bar, drifting & dreaming when Cristi knock-knock-knocked on my bedroom door.

Please, not again. Sleeeeeeep.

"Bacch?"

But her voice dredged me back up. I mumbled for her to come in.

"Are you ok?" she asked, seeing me curled up atop the sheet.

"Just tired."

"Bacch, my parents just called ..."

Her head dropped, shaking back & forth.

"Cristi?"

I motioned for her to sit on the bed, & she did.

"My little hometown might burn down."

"Oh. Oh, shit." I felt like I was still dreaming. "Are they ok?"

"For now." She raised her bloodshot eyes to mine. "Look, I don't like this. I can't stop feeling terrible about the world. I can't talk with you about how I'm feeling, because of how we are, and my feelings involve you, but I have no one else I can talk to, and I don't even know if I can trust you. You know?"

"I know. I'm sorry. You make me want to be the best version of myself. You deserve that. But I'm not at my best. As you can see."

Her hand found mine. Her touch electrified & comforted me, all at once.

"I'm going to protest the executions," she said, "at the stadium."

"Oh."

"I wanted to ask if you'd come with me."

I looked out at the city through the window.

"Look, we're being completely honest with each other, yeah?"

"What is it, Bacch?"

"I'm already going to the executions."

"You are?"

"I have a Servant guest ticket."

She edged away from me, rolled off the bed & stood. No more touch. "Why?"

"I don't support it, you know that. It was just ... a gift."

She hesitated, eyes blank, then shook her head, walked out & closed the door. I could still feel her warm afterglow, the tingles & lingering pressures, from where she'd sat moments before.

We need a home.

God, I need a job.

Cristi

Execution day. Two nights left until eviction. The sky over Sydney was heavy and hazy, oppressing the daylight.

The streets around the stadium were jammed heavier than Friday Night Footy. The light rail there via Anzac Parade still wasn't finished, but The Org had managed to build a massive new bronze statue of Captain Cook between the stadium, Kippax Lake and the Tramway Oval, despite already having one in Hyde Park. Protectors stood guard around the towering figure, his shirt torn, abs and chest gleaming like a colonial Tarzan, a sculpted, bulging groin overlooking us. I walked past, through the car parks. People were lounging in their vans, doors open, drinking and cooking on portable BBQs off the backs of their utes.

The air was getting thicker, smoky.

The sky ... it's biblical.

The asphalt had cracks all throughout, like branches reaching out, overgrowing, with plenty of tiny leaves and petals peeking out.

I hadn't made a sign, to avoid being targeted, in case anything were to happen. Others' signs and chants protested capital punishment, and The Org in general – climate change messages, "Keep Sydney Open" signs, separation of church and state, it all seemed to bubble to the surface out here.

Thou shalt not kill.

Protectors were already pushing protestors back towards Moore Park by the time I got in the thick of it. They were forming groups and lines around us, preparing for something.

I didn't know anyone's name, but we felt united regardless. Solidarity among strangers.

Three Protectors dragged a woman past me, followed by two others ripping up her sign. Tensions were rising.

"For your own protection," called an amplified, official voice, "move away from the stadium and disperse immediately. *For your own protection.*"

Was I wrong to come? Was I wrong to quit The Org? I didn't want to be a dissenter. I didn't want to speak out. It was all so much. The Org. The Protectors. The Servants. The Scouts. The Program. The King.

I just want to live my life, but how?

I was inching through people, scraping shoulders, closer to the stadium now, but keeping off to the sides. Some protestors pushed their way out, moving on, avoiding whatever might come next. Others pushed forward, determined, far too outraged at their government to back down.

The Protectors wore riot gear. From what I had seen, they were the only ones with any weapons. Some protesters had gas masks, water bottles, placards, backpacks … I guess there could be weapons in the backpacks. Bombs, even. *Should I alert the Protectors?*

I had to stay calm, but every protest I'd ever seen on the news ended up as a riot. How was it so inevitable that peaceful protests became riots, every time? Were the protesters the aggressors? The Protectors? I imagined that woman being dragged away on film, on the news … Would it be Org violence against a peaceful protester? Or Protectors doing their job, keeping law and order, in the face of violent riots?

Do you support The Org, or not?

Are you with us, or against us?

Screams arose from the crowd. A huge black armoured Protector vehicle was slowly driving through the crowd, at the front of the protest, near the stadium. Mounted on the front was a huge speaker.

"What is that?" I asked someone next to me.

"Shit," they said. "I think it's an LRAD."

"A what?"

"We're about to get blasted."

People nearby turned and rushed to leave. The armoured vehicle manoeuvred to face out to the masses.

"This is your last chance," called the cold, amplified voice. "Disperse or we will disperse you. The Org does not tolerate riots."

More and more people began moving, but in all different directions now. I tried running further to the side, to escape whatever was coming, to avoid the rush and the crush of humans running scared. It wasn't chaos before, but it was now.

I shouldn't have come by myself. I wondered where Bacch was, up in the stadium, the comfortable seating.

What a prick.

A piercing sound began, getting louder. I couldn't stand it. My ears exploded. My head went dizzy. My stomach churned. People were running, everywhere, falling over, scattering. The Protectors surged forward. That *noise*. I couldn't think, I just ran, my body knocked around by other bodies. I couldn't figure out where to go, how to escape, if it was even possible. I saw blood seeping from someone's ears as they ran past.

People continued to scatter. I ran around the side of the stadium, shoes slamming concrete, weaving through people. At some point the LRAD stopped, or I was far enough away from it. There was also the riotous noise of the stadium to contend with.

Another entrance to the arena appeared, a separate designated entry. Protectors patrolled the area. They saw me and several other dishevelled protesters. They moved towards us. The others scattered. I froze.

The Protectors got closer.

Bacch

There was a separate entrance, away from the protests, just for those associated with The Org. Hari led me through, into The Org wing of the stadium. We were all dressed like a day at the races, suits & sunnies, women with elaborate dresses & even more elaborate hats & headpieces. Injured horses on steroids died every year, executed. Today didn't seem too different. We walked through the belly of the beast, up an incline, until the walkway opened up with a view of the inner stadium.

Our voices were drowned out by everyone else's. The arena was packed. The sky was getting darker, a strange, hazy orange. Cameras were everywhere, every phone held up, filming & livestreaming. Logos & slogans for corporate sponsors were splashed across everything with dazzling vibrancy. Vendors walked up & down the aisles selling sausage sangas & meat pies. Everyone was on their feet. Even those in wheelchairs had been propped up against the railings.

There was no visible sign of a pit anywhere, just the flat field encircled by the grandstands, with a stage in the middle. Advertisements for beers & banks & pharmacies were sprayed on the turf at bizarre, distorted angles, so they show up flat & direct on screen.

Our walkway continued to another level. We went up a few flights of stairs. At a bathroom sign, I asked Hari to wait for me.

"Hurry up," he said, eyes darting. "We gotta find our seats, then I have a quick rendezvous downstairs, the Prayer Hall."

Afterward, as I washed my hands, the tap broke off, separating from the basin as I turned it. I looked for some sign of leaves or vines or other disruptive growth, but there was none. Just a shiny, broken tap. I tried another, which worked. Walking out toward where Hari waited, I saw other doors leading off, personnel warning signs everywhere. I risked a peek through an unlocked double doorway. A corridor stretched on, bending off around the structure, perhaps under the top bleachers, a jumble of wiring & fluoro construction sheets & piping & open ducts & walls without panels & exposed ceiling. They hadn't even finished building the place.

"What are you doing?"

I turned around with a fright, shutting the doors behind me. It was just Hari, but he grabbed my arm.

"You can't snoop around here, brudda," he said.

"Ok, ok. Let's just go."

But Hari didn't go. He led me back to the bathroom, closed the door, took some things from his inner breast pocket, two tiny bags with tiny scoops. He put a scoop from one up his left nostril, and a bigger scoop from the other up his right nostril. Ketamine & cocaine, respectively. I don't really like either, and imagined they'd cancel each other out, but it was my first public execution. I accepted his offerings, head back, nose sucking. We looked at ourselves in the mirror, sniffling.

"I'm scared, man," said Hari.

"Scared? Of what?"

"Everything."

I thought of Cristi. I'd abandoned her. I'd abandoned myself. I put my hand up to the mirror, my reflection doing the same. Could we swap places? No. It was an illusion. This was me. The mirror could break any moment.

"Let's do this."

Cristi

My ears were still ringing as the Protectors approached me. It was difficult to think clearly. The air was hot and the sky seemed suffocated by orange dust. I had to do something. I thought of Bacch.

Please! I ... I work for The Org.

"Excuse me," I said to the Protectors, even stepped towards them. "I'm looking for The Org entrance. I'm in the Program."

"ID," one grunted.

"Cristina!"

Wendy and Patrick were walking towards the stadium entrance, all dolled up in suit and dress and a head ornament like an exploding halo. Patrick scowled. Wendy ran over to me.

"Are you coming in?" she asked.

"Is she with you?" asked the Protectors.

"No," said Patrick.

"Yes," said Wendy. "We work for The Org. C'mon, let's go."

We hurried towards the entrance. Patrick and I didn't acknowledge each other.

"I'm so glad we saw you!" said Wendy, then dropped to a whisper. "I haven't seen you around. I heard you quit."

"No, no, of course not," I said.

"That's a relief. Org staff all get free entry today. They take good care of us, don't they?"

Wendy scanned her Org ID, then Patrick. Both went green. But when I showed mine, the ticket staff didn't let me through.

"Sorry, ma'am," he said. "There seems to be an issue."

My heart pounded. Wendy and Patrick waited for me ahead.

"C'mon, what's going on?" said some people behind us, all glammed up and fired up.

The ticket staff pressed a few buttons. He raised his head. "The Org would like to inform you that you must attend on Monday and report directly to your supervisor. Enjoy the execution."

He handed back my ID. I scuttled through the gate, to Wendy and Patrick. We walked up into the stadium.

Patrick whispered something in my ear.

"What?" I said, grimacing.

"You did quit, didn't you?"

"Just a misunderstanding."

"The Org doesn't tolerate misunderstandings."

"Is that a threat?"

"Just a fact. I'm trying to help you."

"What are you two lovebirds saying?" laughed Wendy.

We stopped speaking. I moved so that Wendy was between us.

"I've been dying to ask you," said Wendy. "How do you know Bacch?"

I didn't want to be here. My escape route had only taken me deeper.

"We're just ... we were ... housemates. That's all."

We emerged upon vast bleachers allocated for those in the Program. The stadium was gigantic.

"How crazy is the sky?" said Wendy.

It was hot and orange and darkening. I checked my phone, and had a missed call, a voice message from Dad. I stopped walking, to listen.

"Hey angel. The fires are much bigger now. We evacuated to the beach, your brother helped. Mum's ok. We're ok. This is God's will. Everything's going to be ok. Hope you're ok. Enjoy the execution, call us later. We love you."

It was ash that had thickened the air. Bushfire smoke, dragged across the land.

I tried to call them, but the call wouldn't connect.

We took our seats. Someone in a white suit and tie was already giving the Welcome to Crown Land and Acknowledgement of The Org, reaffirming that we were on Australian soil, Org soil, sovereign soil, but I couldn't hear them over the frenzied crowd. My ears were still ringing.

Did the Protectors damage my hearing?

The crowd settled and stood for the National Anthem, accompanied by young Org Scouts performing dance routines, all dressed in the same dresses. Border Protection fighter jets flew overhead, leaving trails of smoke behind in the red, white and blue colours of the Australian flag, against the orange-black sky. The crowd boiled over in the excitement until the King and the Vice Servant walked out onto the stage with microphones, surrounded by cameras that projected their faces up on all the screens. Dark blue suits, red ties.

"My ... children!" called the King. "Welcome to this sacred day of justice in the fight against ... terror!"

"Terrorists film their beheadings and publish it for all to see," said the V.S. "What sick world do we live in?"

"Absolutely disgusting ... The only way to fight this barbarianism is to ... do the exact same thing."

"For too long, we have hidden death away from sight, as if we cannot handle this inevitable part of our lives. As if death were not merely another doorway to the Almighty."

"To lose our fear of death ... we must become better acquainted with it ... as a unified people!"

"Let the world know that Australia will not tolerate terrorism!"

The frenzy erupted again as the Casino Three were brought on stage in convict chains, bags over their heads. One was shorter than the other two. The grounds then opened up like an octagonal flower, out from the centre point, with the whirring of sliding mechanics. Inside were wriggling creatures, smooth serpents with sharp fangs, sliding over each other's writhing bodies.

Wendy peered at the snake pit. Patrick was smiling.

To keep up the tension, there was an ad break. All the big sponsors had their turn. Then there were Scouts dressed in the red, white and blue, performing as cheerleaders on raised platforms, with a huge orchestra of saxophones, trumpets, drums, double basses, xylophones, banjos, pianos, piano-key neckties, tubas, harmonicas, wobble boards, percussive scrapers and shakers, all rigged up with microphones and amplifiers, surrounding the snake pit and the terrorists in chains.

"Ladies and gentlemen ... Now is the moment you've all been waiting foooor!" The King's voice carried through the air like the voice of God, deep and booming through every amplifier. It had taken on a new resonance, a new confidence. Beads of sweat hung from his forehead. The King was in a fervour.

"We have drawn global criticism for our treatment of asylum seekers, Australian children in regional youth detention, Indigenous people, queers and terrorists!"

The crowds booed and jeered, whether in support or in dissidence I could not tell.

"But we are a STRONG nation! We are an INDEPENDENT, FREE nation!"

The booming voice was everywhere, as if trying to drown any sense of indignation.

"We will decide who dies in this country, and the circumstances in which they die!"

At that moment, one of the tall prisoners tried to run, but his feet were shackled. He fell, head still covered by the black bag, and began to crawl. The Protectors grabbed him and removed the black hood to reveal a wide-eyed, dishevelled, terrified human being. They grabbed his chains and dragged him back. They forced him to stand, before pushing him into the snake pit.

You couldn't hear the screams above those of the crowd. Confetti cannons went off everywhere. I couldn't even see the pit that well anymore, but the cameras projected close-ups on all the screens, displaying the man being bitten from all angles by the animals. He clawed at the walls of the pit. The more he kicked and swatted, the more vicious the snakes became. He even tried to kill a few with his bare hands, but the mixed venom of several native species slowed him down, his twitches fading.

He died. Cheers and applause.

The Protectors removed the hood of the shorter one. It seemed to be a young girl. I screamed, and my hands covered my mouth.

"What's wrong?" asked Wendy.

The girl was Bacch's friend.

It was Ria.

Cheers and applause.

Bacch

It was pretty ruthless, watching a guy get eaten alive by snakes in a stadium. The sky above churned red.

Hari hadn't returned the whole time. I'd been speaking with a Servant, dark blue suit, red tie, streaks of silver through otherwise deep black hair, standing against the railing, looking out at it all.

"The Colosseum!" he shouted, as the terrorist's convulsions stopped. Everyone on our viewing platform echoed with glee. Including me. Amongst The Org, it felt necessary to show your devotion, to display your enthusiasm, to be with us, not against us.

"Bacch, what a strange name," he said. "Like the composer?"

"Yeah," I said, feeling slippery, acting sober. "But my dad spelled it wrong. So, more like *bacchanalia*."

"Huh. I prefer that. I'm Burton. What do you do, Bacch?"

"I'm an ... entrepreneur."

"What kind of business?"

"Food retail ... and private education. But, I'd like to ..."

My heartbeat throbbed through me.

"Bacch?" said Burton, peering at me.

"I'd like to join The Org. Plus, I'm having some housing issues."

He laughed. "Let's hit the bar, while your friend Hari's still gone."

"You know Hari?"

He didn't answer, just walked ahead. We joined a few other Servants, dresses & suits, ordering drinks, chatting.

"The riots were squashed pretty quickly ..."

"It's remarkable they still bother ..."

Cristi. Was she ok? Some notion of how badly I'd fucked up began to worm its way into my brain. I moved to leave, to call her, check she was ok, away from earshot. Burton's blue suit stopped me in my tracks. He passed me a whiskey mix on ice. I needed a drink.

"Praise The Org!" he called, putting his glass up in salute.

"Praise The Org!" everyone repeated, including me, clinking, cheers.

If I just say the exact opposite of what I believe in, I might flourish here.

"Why can't they just protest peacefully?" said another Servant. "They'd be easier to ignore."

"I hate when people try to question the system," I said. "It's there for a reason, right?"

"Right, right!"

"I mean, they just don't see what we see!" I continued. "We're progressing our country forward by keeping its beliefs backwards!"

"Right! Wait ..."

"The non-believers just want chaos & lawlessness, they want anarchy, they want equality & drugs."

"Right!"

"Maybe they'd all better start working for this country, working for The Org."

"Right! Right!"

"Fuck em all! Fuck em! Fuck those ..."

As I spewed out each slur, I felt sicker & sicker. My voice was carried off from me as I said these things. I won't write down the rest of it. It wasn't me. What was me?

Please ... I'm nobody ...

They cheered me on & we drank. I've never had that many men in white collars smile approvingly at me before.

"Praise The Org!"

The Servants screamed it with me, finished their drinks, and we went again. When we returned to the viewing platform for the next

execution, a few of the Servants slapped me on the back, grinning &
slurping.

"The kid speaks his mind."

"You'd do well at The Org."

"Gotta show him the prayer room."

"Keep in touch, see how we can help."

"Imagine this cunt on radio ..."

It was difficult to walk. I wasn't used to ketamine, and with the
quick drinks on top, it felt like my limbs might float away from me
instead of keeping me walking like a normal, law-abiding, devoted Org
member.

"You right?" asked Burton.

"Splendiddddd."

He passed me his contact card, said he worked for the Servant of
Bureaucracy. Another pat on the back.

Hari still hadn't returned. I didn't know where Cristi was. I wasn't
taking much notice of the snake pit or the stage – they'd moved on to
more ad breaks anyway. The sky had become a bizarre cloud of burning
red. The air was thick. *What's going on?* That notion, that terrible feeling
seeped through me again. I gulped at my drink, and looked out across
the stadium. At the terrorists.

At ... Ria.

The dread erupted in me. I felt sick, poisoned, incapable.

How does this happen?

It was her. It was the wrong person. It was obvious, yet no one
seemed to see it. The evidence was standing right there, chained &
shaking. What had she already been through? I couldn't imagine. I
looked to Burton, chatting with the others, and looked back at the stage,
immobile.

They were blaming – *killing* – the wrong person.

Cristi

They brought Ria forward. The sky. The air. People were coughing all around us, ash falling, while others put face masks on.

"Surely she's not a terrorist," I said, standing in my seat. "She's just a girl!"

"I hear that kids as young as ten are into it," said Patrick.

It was too loud, too thick. I was off balance, ears ringing, light-headed. I sat down again.

"Ladies and gentlemen!" called the amplified King.

I wanted to vomit, cry, save her, escape, but my body was paralysed.

As if to overwhelm me further, screams and crunching metal and a heavy impact reverberated through the stadium. Across from where we sat, part of the bleachers suddenly disappeared, collapsed, over in the cheap seats. My breath caught in my throat. A plume of debris and ash arose in its place.

The musicians stopped. The crowds murmured. The stadium was caught in a momentary precipice, the red sky descending. Then people began rushing to the exits, trying to breathe through masks and screams.

"Terrorist attack!" some shouted.

The entire stadium seemed to shake in its foundations. Hordes of humans were scrambling, especially around the collapsed grandstands. The King just continued as if the place wasn't falling down around him. I couldn't see Ria anymore.

I expected vines and trees to explode out of the wreckage, like at the casino, but there were none. No wild foliage. No growth. Just a lack of structural integrity.

"We need to go," I said.

The three of us shared quick glances before moving to the exits. But there were too many people, and we were soon stuck. I looked around for another escape route. Even here, The Org wing had cracks in the columns, exposed wiring sticking out. We just hadn't noticed it before. We'd been too excited, too distracted.

"Come with me!" said Patrick. He grabbed my hand and pulled.

"Hey!" I pulled back, but he didn't let go. I realised he was holding Wendy's hand, too.

"I know another way," he shouted.

We squirmed out of the bottleneck of bodies. Patrick led us up some stairs.

"We can go through the Servant level," he yelled as we ran. "The Prayer Hall."

I sucked in air, forgetting to breathe for so long. The stairs seemed to betray gravity. The dizziness had only gone deeper. At least my ears weren't bleeding.

I thought of Bacch. I saw an apparition of him, collapsed in the stairwell, through the delirium. Was it really him? I couldn't know anything for sure anymore.

Bacch

I am way too fucked up for this.

Some Servants were watching the chaos, from the platform, behind the glass. Others were making nervous phone calls. Burton had disappeared. I wobbled to the bar, clinging to the counter for fear of drifting away.

"Do you know what's going on out theeeeeeeere?" I asked the bartender.

"Nah, I just make the drinks."

So I ordered a double & called Hari. He didn't answer. I called Cristi. No answer.

The drink was ready.

"Where's the Prayer Hall?" I asked.

He explained how to get there. I finished the double & dragged my body onward. It wasn't far, just down one flight of stairs. I stumbled on the first few steps before tripping & hitting my face. I looked up to see the closed double doors to the Prayer Hall.

And Cristi.

And Wendy.

And Patrick.

Through the delirium. Was it really Cristi? I couldn't know anything for sure anymore.

I am way too –

"Bacch!"

Cristi was coming up the stairs, and almost tripped, too, but I reached out & eased her fall. We fell into a little heap on the stairs as the stadium went wild around us. We pulled further into each other's uncomfortable embrace, disfigured on the steps. I was crying. She wasn't.

"We need to go," she said.

We helped each other up, wrapped in each other's arms, and joined Wendy & Patrick. They both looked at us.

"Let's just go," said Patrick, taking Wendy's hand. He scanned his ID on the lock of the double doors. I didn't think he would have access, just a Program member. But the doors opened up.

The Prayer Hall. What a sight.

Servants & whoever else were all dancing & drinking & smoking, spread out across the chamber. Some languished together upon a spinning lazy Susan, food smeared everywhere. Others wore absurdly decorated masquerades, peacock feathers spraying out from their heads, with nothing below. Fucking each other & pouring magnums of Penfolds Grange Hermitage all over themselves. No enforcement of The Org's bonk ban. Naked trapeze artists danced from swinging ceiling pendulums. Lions roared & acrobats soared. The lions were heavily chained. Two Servants were doing doggy on a pile of MO newspapers. Others just laughed at each other's jokes & poured more wine into their overflowing cups. The tightropes above had been stretched so thin that the tightrope walkers were falling & breaking themselves below. They lay there, screaming & writhing. No one helped, just kept drinking & talking shit.

We'd apparently interrupted a celebration of some kind.

I recognised certain Servants. Lines were vacuumed from the front bench by elected noses. The Speaker could not speak, due to his mouth being occupied by someone else's private parts. I saw Hari, his suit askew, drifting between a few people. A circus with no ringmaster to lead anyone. This was just how it was. A horrific sight, in all. They didn't even see us. They didn't even hear us. They just kept up the Org orgy.

"DAD?" screamed Patrick.

He was staring at a man with his pants down, embroiled with Hari.

"Hari!"

"Bacch!"

"Patrick?" said the man, grabbing at his trousers.

"Hari," I said, grabbing him. "Wild shit is going on. The building isn't safe. We gotta go."

"Mate," said Hari, eyes glazed, off his head. "Nowhere is safe. Every day of life, you risk losing it."

"We gotta go, brudda."

"Dad, what the fuck?" lamented Patrick.

"I'm working, son ..."

"We gotta go," I repeated.

Hari shook me off. "I'm not going anywhere. You're either fully dedicated, or not at all. I need to get back to work, Bacch. You should join us, though."

We stared into each other's intoxicated eyes. Was he serious? Or was it just for show while in the lion's den?

"*EVACUATE NOW,*" screamed an alarm suddenly. "*YOUR BUILDING IS ON FUCKING FIRE. PLEASE EVACUATE NOW, OR YOU MIGHT DIE. WHY DOES NO ONE EVER TAKE ME SERIOUSLY ...*"

"Bacch!" screamed Cristi over the alarm.

Wendy pulled Patrick across the chamber, dodging the unholy revelry.

Cristi grabbed me. I stumbled away from Hari, as he fell backwards, smiling, into the writhing pit of bodies.

Cristi

We escaped down several flights of service stairs and through an unfinished corridor, running past wires and panels and construction signs. We barged out of a side door and joined the heaving mass of people getting out the entrance. Bacch and I spilled outside and ran, Patrick and Wendy following. The red sky had sunk close to the ground. We were coughing and eventually all stopped for breath near Kippax Lake, in the grass between the stadium and bustling Anzac Parade. Protectors were still everywhere, but instead of helping people, most were stamping their boots on the plants that had grown even larger through the asphalt of the carparks.

Bacch held my hand. Wendy held Patrick's. We all looked at each other through the red haze, alarms and horns and screams all swept up in the wind, swirling our hair and dresses. Wendy's headpiece had somehow stayed on her head, but barely. Patrick helped her readjust it. The clouds were dark above. Ash fell like burned snow.

"I just wanna go home," said Wendy.

"Will you be ok?" I asked.

"We'll be fine," said Patrick.

"See you at work on Monday?" said Wendy.

"Of course. Of course."

They walked towards the road, comforting each other.

"Fuck that guy," said Bacch.

I grabbed him, hugged him, unable to let go. He fell into my arms. Bacch started coughing, choking on the red air. I had to clear my throat too, and we separated. Sirens were everywhere, getting closer, getting louder. People were still fleeing nearby, crossing the pedestrian walkway over Anzac into Moore Park West. We joined them. We dodged cars crossing South Dowling, and followed the light rail construction up Devonshire Street. Almost home.

Only, it wasn't home. We were getting evicted.

"We should throw a demolition party," said Bacch, as we stumbled together through the leafy backstreets of Surry Hills.

The rest can burn.

I called my parents, and finally got through. They were ok for now, evacuated to the beach.

"Cristina," said Dad. "We're concerned. We received a call, from The Org. Your supervisor, Mrs Ogglesworth."

"Um ... why?"

"She said you'd quit and disappeared. Said you vandalised The Org park? She was worried. We're worried, on top of everything else right now. We said, have you called the dorms? She said you don't live at the dorms. Where have you been living, Cristina? Why have you been lying to us? What's going on with you?"

My throat stuck.

"Cristina?"

How could I explain any of it?

"Cristina, are you still there?"

I don't know. I don't know.

"Cristi–"

"I like girls. And I like boys."

Silence.

"Look," I hurried on. "I'm going into The Org to clear everything up. I'll fix it. I'll try to move into the dorms on Sunday. Everything will be ok."

"You're not on the run, then?"

"No. I'm safe."

"Ok. Well ... we love you."

"I love you, too."

We could do nothing more than pray while the fires raged.

Bacch

We threw a demolition party the next night. Saturday night. Our final night.

During the arvo, I went up & down the stairs of the building, inviting everyone. I was about to knock on Jeffrey's door when I got a call back from Kafi.

"She's gone."

"What?"

"Even Ria's lawyer disappeared, bro. Their record of her is wrong. She's officially someone else. We don't know if that was her at the ... the ... stadium ... if she survived ... No one knows what's going on, bro ..."

My heart sank. I sat down on the creaky steps of the apartment building.

"We tried to make a complaint of misidentification this morning, but it would have to be approved by the Servant for Bureaucracy, which could take years, they said, even decades. Bro ... they've lost my sister."

"Surely ... surely we can do something."

"Maybe I can find her, from the inside. Work for The Org, and rescue her. Maybe ..."

"Well ..." I ventured, feeling guilty. "I'm joining The Org."

"You won't keep tutoring, then?"

"I still want to tutor you. And ... Ria."

"Nah. You were never that good at it anyway, bro."

"You were the one always napping."

"See? You're defensive, instead of receptive. Not good for a teacher."

"Well, at least you've learnt a few things."

He sighed. "I just wanted to drink goon on the beach with a girl ..."

We said our farewells. I didn't yet know how The Org worked – does anyone? – but I promised him I'd try to find info on Ria. From the inside.

"I'm gonna change things, Kafi. I'm really gonna change things."

Neither of us seemed convinced, but there was nothing more to say. I felt sick. I needed a drink.

Most of the building came up that night. Even Mrs Clancy made it. Jeffrey carried her up the stairs & Cristi followed with her IV stand. Mrs Clancy had more in common with the trees than I'd realised. Her daughter was arriving the next day to take her to a nursing home. She didn't seem pleased. Jeffrey still hadn't organised a place, and was considering just booking a one-way flight somewhere. But he had no passport & no money. Regardless, his optimism persisted. The broken teeth made his smile glow somehow brighter. Must have been all the sugar.

The city was still smothered. The sky was still ash. Cristi's parents were ok. Their home was ok. Other homes were not, and fires still blazed across the land, across the sky.

I'd bought a few spray cans for us to experiment with on the walls. Cristi got right into it. She didn't actually depict anything, no discernible image other than wherever her hand went. The stereo was turned up. Her eyes were closed. Her hand danced across the living room walls in huge arches & erratic splats of choreography. Her waist moved with the music. Her colour-stained hand moved with her heart.

Oscar, the young fella from the bakery, brought over bags full of the wildest assortment of baked goods I'd yet seen. He ended up deep in conversation with a war widower who lived downstairs. They spoke to no one else for the rest of the night until they began kissing & left together. Jeffrey was frothing on the lamingtons. Mrs Clancy tried her shaky hand at graffiti art. Shaky lines. It was an interesting style.

Hari came over. We went to the kitchen. He microwaved a plate.

"How are you doing, brudda?" he asked.

"Were you ok, after we left? At the stadium?"

He nodded. The microwave beeped. He put the plate on the counter, tapped out some of his baggie & cut up some lines.

"I can't stick around," he said. "Got another party afterwards. You want this?"

"I'm not really feeling ... The Org drug tests, I think."

"They don't test me, thankfully."

He racked both lines, head back. "You tell me how the induction goes, brudda. Keep me in the loop. Keep me informed, yeah?"

"Um, sure, man."

"Ah! WE NEED TO INDULGE!"

I grabbed him for a hug, held it. But then we separated & rejoined the party. At one point I heard the *CRACK* & *WHOOOOSH* of a nang in the bathroom. Hari walked out, drifting as if on the moon, breathing in & out of the balloon of nitrous oxide.

"Are there any more balloons?" asked Mrs Clancy.

Hari giggled. "Whatever you want, baby."

Bianca & her boyfriend, Federico, arrived. They danced barefoot in the bare living room while tenants sat around eating the pastries. But soon Jeffrey took Mrs Clancy back downstairs & everyone said thank you for the farewell, it had been nice to know everyone. Mrs Clancy made us all add her on socials before she left. Cristi & I became two of her seven followers.

"Last night," Hari was telling me at the door, "a guy pissed in his own mouth at the urinal in the club, got everyone to watch & film, live streaming the stream. Everything is absurd, man."

Hari finished his last drink.

"Everything is absurd."

And he was gone.

Bianca & Federico stayed awhile. It was good to see her. They were still in an open relationship & wanted us four to all get in bed together. Cristi wasn't keen.

"I thought this was a demolition party," said Bianca. "No one's demolishing anyone."

So she & Federico left too, and then it was just Cristi & me, our final night in the apartment, a wasteland of baked goods & spontaneous graffiti murals, barely anything of our own left. We curled up together on the balcony. Our spot. Magic amidst the damage. It was a beautiful city sometimes, if you could somehow push back the intruding thoughts of disappearances & executions & bushfires & broken families. Was Ria ok? Was she coping? Toeing the line? Escaped?

I looked at Cristi, and she back at me. Her eyes offered the world knowing full well they couldn't give it. But I didn't want the world. I wanted her. What was the difference? Our noses played with each other. Everything rose up like a revolution against the melancholic mania, so long rooted in my marrow.

"Does this city even want us here?" she murmured.

"I want you here."

We kissed, finally, and the stakes of existence seemed so much higher. My wrath at the world seemed wasted as I disappeared into a state in which we might have died & slipped away, where everything is suddenly understood just a lil too late. Cristi exposed everything I'd hidden away. My heart swam in a sea of snakes. Tipped with poison, heavy with hope.

Some moments just carry you & your words & your world away.

Cristi

Cities steal the stars.

Look at the sky – nothing.

Look at the city. It's like they all fell.

We both knelt on my bed, facing each other, touching each other. I wasn't sure of our future, Bacch and I. He was even more of a lost puppy than me. Besides, I had so much to explore. I could have women, who felt like me, who could teach me different things. I could be anyone. Anyone.

But, after everything, for our final night in that vandalised, stripped apartment, teetering up there in that savage skyline, heading into uncertainty, we loved each other for everything that we'd been through, everything we'd shared. I allowed myself to feel what I had to feel, even if it would never last. We slid each other's clothes off with gentle movements, looking in our eyes, bewildered, hungry, beautiful. We were naked together and it didn't feel like that day with the Protectors. We pressed our skin together and couldn't stop. I allowed him to spread my bare legs with his hands as he moved lower, kissing along my ribs, down my belly. I ached as he spread my lips with his finger, his mouth. I gripped his hair and moaned. All the walls we'd kept up, in fear of the feeling taking over, all just crumbled, as we did, into a billion grains of sand, and even more drops in the ocean, even more suns in the universe, even more atoms in your heart. The human race, here and gone before the gods even finish a breath.

The world really had flipped on its head.

We were among the stars.

We demolished each other.

Bacch

It was Sunday & I was hungover. Cristi might have been, too. We were out of time. The day of eviction. I needed an Org ID to secure rooms at the dorms, if there were any available. But we had it figured out. I'd called Burton the day before, pleaded for a referral. He'd granted it, but said that I owed him.

Cristi & I walked out of the vast ground foyer of The Org, fresh plastic ID in hand, out the giant doors & toward the dorms, past the manicured lawns & IV trees, thriving in spite of the apocalyptic air. The only thing out of place was a jacaranda tree growing up through the centre of one of the pavement slabs, purple petals in full bloom. We stepped around the trunk & roots & crumbling concrete. Protectors would deal with it soon enough.

Entering the dorms, I signed in to The Org network, to get mobile service, using my new ID.

Join us.

The receptionist was the same as last time. I had to play it cool. We asked about rooms.

"I think I've seen you before," she said, eyeing me.

"That must have been *nobody*. Me, I'm *somebody*. I have an identity. Look." I showed her my Org ID.

"You are correct." She scanned our IDs. "We have rooms available, certainly. The Org is here to take you in. You'll be in separate wings, of course, unless you're husband and wife?"

The mad thought occurred to propose to Cristi, right there & then, make her parents happy, make my parents happy, make The Org happy.

"No," said Cristi. "Just friends."

"I can approve your application, Bacch, as it seems your registration with the Program is complete. You still need to visit The Org so they can set you up with Inductions. Cristina, you'll need to report to your supervisor before I can approve your room."

"Can I do that on a Sunday?" asked Cristi. She was tense. "I thought The Org didn't work on holy days."

"I'm working," the receptionist shrugged. "Life, like faith, is full of paradox. They say intelligence is the ability to hold two opposing views at the same time."

"Intelligence can be many things," said Cristi.

The receptionist tapped her red pen on the blue desk & told us to go back to The Org to clear things up. Then, perhaps, we could move our belongings in that evening, ready for a fresh start on Monday.

We walked back into the hazy heat, returning to The Org, around the jacaranda, past the IV trees.

"Cristi, hey ..."

We stopped at the towering entrance doors. We held each other, looked at each other. Her angelic face had gone stern, but she gave me her softness, her lips. The world didn't deserve her. I didn't deserve her.

My phone buzzed. We parted & I checked – it was Mum.

"Let's meet down here after you see your supervisor," I said. "I'll sort this Inductions thing."

"Hey," said Cristi. "Be careful."

We shared a final, beautiful glance. I answered the phone, as Cristi disappeared inside The Org. As the doors closed, I noticed vines growing up the building from the ground, only a few feet up, but moving quickly, getting thicker in front of my eyes.

"Bacch? How's the sky looking down in Sydney there?"

"Pretty hectic, Mum. Any fires near you?"

"No, not so far. The sky is wild, though." *Sip.* "How've you been, my love?"

"I got a job. Working for The Org, in the Program. Cristi & I had to move to the dorms."

"Oh! You're working for The Org?"

"Yeah, Mum."

"Is it ... what you want to be doing?"

"Gotta try everything once."

"You don't, though."

"Look, Mum, tell Dad I'm working for The Org. He'll be proud. I'll do you both proud."

Sip. Gulp.

"I know you will, honey. I know you will."

Cristi

I looked behind me as The Org doors closed, as Bacch disappeared behind them.

It was eerie to be here on a Sunday. Only a few officials walked through the foyer, unlike the usual weekday bustle. The sounds of my own steps seemed heightened as I approached the dark blue front desk.

"Hello. Praise The Org. I've been requested to check in with my supervisor. I'm not sure if I can today, but it's urgent."

The receptionist looked up my name. She seemed to hesitate, peering between me and the screen. She typed a few things.

"Please, take a seat," she said. "They'll come for you shortly."

I'd barely sat down when two men in suits approached me. They greeted me with dutiful apathy and led me toward one of the many elevator doors. If they were Servants, they were a different breed. Inside, as the doors closed, one scanned his ID. A panel opened to reveal more floor numbers. He pressed one. The elevator began going *down*, not up.

Why, that's where The Org keeps the troublemakers.

Begin the strip searches.

"Am I going to speak with Mrs Ogglesworth?" I asked, clenching my fists.

No reply.

Bacch

Cristi was nowhere in sight as I entered the foyer, walking past the climbing, thickening vine branches.

Already in her meeting.

I followed the receptionist's instructions, up the elevator, down some corridors to another reception desk. They took me to a grey carpeted interview room. No pot plants anywhere. They sat me in a chair & left.

My future with Cristi played out in my mind over those few minutes, unravelling. I imagined trees, towering forests, giant lungs of oxygen & carbon dioxide, intertwined with human lungs, no nutrient bags, no IV drips. I imagined Cristi dancing, barefoot in the grass, letting go yet connecting. I imagined us, together, teaching ourselves everything we didn't yet know, fighting through the madness of the world.

The door opened, and a man in a suit appeared, closed the door & sat across from me.

"Hello, Bacch," he said, placing a screen on the table, opening files. "I'm from Inductions. You'll start your induction week tomorrow, praise The Org, but let's get you set up first."

"Hello, sir."

"So, you're a believer?"

"Um ..."

"Yes, of course you are. You've never had sexual relations with another man?"

"Umm ..."

217

Did he sense my hesitation? Can they read the signals? Is their recognition AI monitoring my physiology?

"No," I said. "Of course not."

"Hmm. Bacch, we're going to provide you with a daily prescription."

"Of what?"

"Nothing nasty, of course. We just want you operating at your best here at The Org."

"Ok ..."

"Do you have any questions so far?"

"Where is ... may I please see the prayer room?"

"Um ... why?"

"I am devout."

"You want to pray now? Why not here?"

"Well, what's the point of the prayer rooms then?"

He tapped his pen and shifted in his seat. "I believe the prayer room on this level is currently ... occupied."

Silence.

"Anyway," he continued, "we see you studied some digital marketing. A role in the Program has opened up, in the Public Relations Sector. You'd fit well."

"Did someone leave?"

The man smiled. "You don't leave The Org. You're either fully dedicated, or not at all. Which are you, Bacch?"

I expected it to ring hollow. I thought my voice might crack. I'd be found out as a sham, a filthy addict, a traitor. But this was survival. I had to believe.

"Praise The Org," I said. "*Praise The Org.*"

His cheeks twitched with approval. "Welcome, Bacch."

Cristi

The elevator doors opened up to a wide corridor with endless doorways. This was not New Parliament House. We were deeper. The men's boots clicked against the tiling. There was nothing natural down here. No plants, no outside light. We were underground. The sky could stay red forever. Down here, you'd never know.

They took me through a door into a sparse interview room. Or – *interrogation room*. My heart backflipped. I wanted to run away from it all, but I couldn't. They motioned to a seat on one side of the table. I sat. They took my phone and ID, then disappeared and closed the door.

I was trapped in the very foundations of The Org, of my country.

A few minutes passed, I think. I wasn't sure of time. I had to clear this up, once and for all. Swear my allegiance. My mind saw Bacch. I imagined myself, allowed to return to the world upstairs, hugging him in the foyer, face in his hair, smelling his closeness, walking out, toward our new home, a young, confused couple on the verge of living our lives, experimenting with possibility, serving The Org. It was everything I'd ever wanted.

The door opened, and a Servant walked in, silver streaks through black hair, plain blue suit, red tie, lines beneath his eyes.

"Good afternoon," he said, sitting across from me. The chair legs scraped against the floor. "I work for the Servant for Bureaucracy. Cristina, you were in Public Relations before you quit, correct?"

"Actually, sir," I said. "That's what I wanted to talk to you about."

He placed a screen in front of him, looking things up. The previous men walked in. One put a prescription bottle on the table and a white plastic cup of water. The other placed a large, white Bible on the table. They each bore The Org crest. The men left and closed the door.

"Cristina, we know you've been finding things … difficult. We're here to help. Take one of these, once daily."

"What is it?"

"Nothing nasty of course. We just want you operating at your best. Take one, now."

"The Org is against drugs. Are you saying –"

"Remember, Cristina. There are *legal* drugs, and *illegal* drugs. The Org says these drugs are ok. So, they are."

I hesitated, but there seemed no other choice. I unscrewed the cap, popped a pill and washed it down.

"So, Cristina. Why did you unplug the tree on Level 73?"

Was it a truth serum? Was he going to extract all of my misdeeds and rebellious notions and thoughts about women and sex and escape? But no, I'd only just swallowed.

"I was upset," I said.

"That's all?"

"I just want to see some trees that aren't hooked up and surviving off drips. Don't you?"

The man sighed, tapping a red pen on the desk. "We have to keep you here, Cristina. At least for the next few days. Perhaps weeks, or months, or … well, we know you've been questioning things – the world, The Org, questioning yourself, even. We have loyal eyes, in the Program, everywhere."

Patrick?

"We also have answers," he continued. "The Org has answers."

"Please …" I stammered.

"You can't just stir up dissent like that, Cristina. Unplugging our beautiful trees."

"Please, I want to be loyal. I want to apologise. I want to work again. I just want to live my life."

He took a long breath through his nostrils, almost sucking me up with it.

"You attended the stadium protest," he finally said.

I hung my head.

He tapped his pen.

I was silent.

"You don't just quit The Org, you see. We move you to a new sector. Down here. For as long as it takes."

"Please, no ..."

"You'll learn, Cristina. We all do. The Org has the answers. Praise The Org. Praise The Org."

Bacch

Tears welled as I walked out, clenching my verified Org ID & a prescription. I'd done it. I had to befriend the snakes inside me, no matter how venomous. I tried looking around & appreciating everything I saw. There wasn't much to see, but it helped.

I waited for Cristi in the vast foyer, looking out at the IV trees & that rogue jacaranda through the windows. I imagined us snuggling together on a beach, beyond the endless cities, beneath palm trees, all natural, no drips, watching the ocean lick the shoreline with a hypnotic rhythm, hearing the gentle crash, sparkling & stretching forever north & south. The world was empty but for us. As I daydreamed, we fell deeper into the land, which was not sandy but smooth, not compact but yielded to our movements, as we kissed & fell further into each other, into a billion grains, and even more drops of the ocean, even more stars in the universe, even more atoms in your heart.

I'm gonna change things, Ria. I'm really gonna change things.

The vines had reached the windows. They grew impossibly fast. Looking further, I saw more jacaranda trees, already blooming at waist height & still growing, breaking through pavement, a dizzying purple in the ashy air. The other windows around the foyer were now covered in branches or blocked by rusty figs & eucalypts, growing at a similar pace. I thought of the casino.

Was it happening again? Giant vines and towering trees to take us all down? To destroy the pylons of city skyscrapers, to swallow the Harbour Bridge whole, to overgrow Town Hall and smother it with wattle bushes, to

send rivers flowing down Elizabeth Street, mangroves lining the sidewalks,
crawling up shopfronts?

To destroy The Org?

I shook my head. Surely the paranoia had become too much. I was losing it. I had to be protected from my own thoughts. The Org knew; we couldn't trust our own minds. The only thing that could save us now was The Org itself. Only the Protectors could protect us from ourselves, from nature itself.

I was with us, not against us.

Praise The Org.

I was sweating.

Praise The Org.

Cracks appeared in the shiny floor.

Praise The Org.

The receptionist was eyeing me.

Praise The Org.

Cristi hadn't returned.

Praise The Org.

This was survival.

Praise The Org.

I had to believe.

Praise The Org.

I'm really gonna change things ...

Praise The Org.

Praise The Org.

Praise The Org.

Cristi

The End ...

Acknowledgements

Thank you to my mum. A mother isn't the ideal first reader, especially with this kind of content. But her feedback helped redirect me when I most needed it. Thanks, Mum and Dad, for everything.

Thank you to my other early readers for your valuable time and feedback – James, Lauren, Manks, Penny, Chamira, Scott, Lou and Faf (and thanks Aisha for your blurb insights!).

Thank you to my editor, Katie Kearns. You were the first professional I ever showed this to. I'm forever grateful for your insight and professionalism, especially in dealing with a first-time author, with delicate subject matter.

Thank you to Scott Marsh, one of Australia's best visual artists. Thank you for being so responsive and letting me use your artwork for my debut novel cover.

Scott's work is sharply political, comical, and iconically Australian. This, alongside his talent depicting native wild flowers and plants (as appear in the novel), and the subversive nature of graffiti art itself, made it the perfect match. Please support his work.

Thank you Nada Backovic, my designer. I felt supported throughout the whole process as a first-timer. I couldn't have found a more exceptional professional to bring the cover and interior to life, and to help guide me through the crucial final stages.

Thank you to all the artists who dealt with me on lyric permissions – DJ Eddie Amador, Roland Clark, Dino Lenny, Doorly, Cadence Weapon via Kelp Management, and Jacques Greene via Sony Music Publishing. If you like house music or raving, please support them.

Thank you to the publishers and agents who either rejected or never got back to me. It led me down a more fulfilling path.

Thank you, for reading.

If you liked this …

K.J. Hennessy is currently working on a spicy fantasy series where magic, uni, AI, romance, regional Australia and the potential for WWIII all collide.

In the meantime …

Say hi!

K.J. Hennessy loves to interact with fellow readers and writers.
Say hi via most social media: @kjhennessy.x
or via email: kjhennessy.x@gmail.com

For author updates, feel free to join the community by signing up to the mailing list.

Review
As a debut novelist, your review is hugely beneficial and helps a lot with visibility during these early days. Hit up Goodreads, Amazon or wherever else you get your books.

Thank you all so much!

www.ingramcontent.com/pod-product-compliance
Lightning Source LLC
Chambersburg PA
CBHW030623120726
47904CB00006B/2014